Echoes

Jem Duducu

For WRW, Sandy, Jake and Oliver

1st Edition 2019

All rights reserved. No part of this publication may be reproduced, transmitted or stored in a retrieval system in any form or by any means without the permission in writing from the author. This book is the sole intellectual rights of the author. Echoes is a work of fiction and any similarities to people, characters or events either in the past or present is purely coincidental.

Also by the author:

History Titles

The Busy Person's Guide to British History

The British Empire in 100 Facts

Deus Vult: A Concise History of the Crusades

The Napoleonic Wars in 100 Facts

The Romans in 100 Facts

Forgotten History: Unbelievable Moments from the Past

The American Presidents in 100 Facts

The Sultans: The Rise and Fall of the Ottoman Rulers and Their World: A 600-Year History

Historical Fiction Titles

Silent Crossroads

Other Media

@jemduducu - Twitter

History Gems - Facebook

Neon - podcast

Condensed History Gems - podcast

Glossary of Terms

A-O - Area of Operation

APC - Armored Personnel Carrier

ARVN - Army of the Republic of Vietnam (South), the regime supported by America

Charlie - Derogatory term for Vietnamese

Cherry - New Recruit

Claymore - Directional anti-personnel mine fired by remote control, shooting metal balls

Contact - A fight between American and Vietnamese soldiers, varying greatly in size and intensity

Dink - Derogatory term for Vietnamese

DMZ - Demilitarized Zone, the border area between North and South Vietnam

DSC - Distinguished Service Cross, US Army medal awarded for bravery in combat

Free Fire Zone - An area where anyone unidentified is considered an enemy combatant

FNG - Fucking New Guy

Frag - Military slang for a hand grenade; also, to deliberately kill with a hand grenade

FUBAR - Fucked Up Beyond All Recognition

Gook - Derogatory term for Vietnamese

Hooch - Thatched hut

K-bar - The standard infantry combat knife

LeRP/LRP - Long Range Patrol

LZ - Landing Zone for a helicopter

Medevac - Amalgamation of the words Medical Evacuation from a conflict zone by air transport, usually helicopter

MP - Military Police

NCO – Non-commissioned officer, someone who has risen through the ranks

NVA - North Vietnamese Army, regular soldiers from North Vietnam

Pig - Nickname for the M60 heavy machine gun

Punji sticks - Sharpened bamboo stakes, tipped with poison or excrement, set in a camouflaged pits

RPG - Rocket-propelled grenade, sometimes called a bazooka

SNAFU - Situation Normal, All Fucked Up

VC - Viet Cong, communist guerrillas in South Vietnam

Tom Moretti had never felt so alive. He knew the enemy was out there, and his brain worked overtime as he tried to interpret the thick jungle even though he couldn't see ten feet in front of him. His eyes strained to filter the soft lines of nature from the stark edges of man-made weapons. The occasional shriek of a monkey, the call of a bird, the rustling of leaves and the incessant ticks and clicks of countless insects bombarded his ears, but it was his own heavy breathing he heard. Surely it was the ultimate irony that a place so full of life also threatened death, probably his.

As a child, he had seen the jungle in Tarzan movies, and he had imagined it smelled sweet and clean, like freshly cut grass, but he had been wrong. The jungle smelled of dirt - thick, wet earth - and rotting things so decomposed they were indistinguishable from plant or animal. Now, nine months into his tour, he had grown accustomed to the smell, just as he had become accustomed to the fact that he, too, smelled ... stank in fact. Days in the bush had stripped the veneer of civilization from the savage he had become.

His body itched with sweat and his drab olive green uniform clung to him. He could feel a trickle of perspiration edge down his face and neck to pool in the groove made by his collarbone. He wiped it away absentmindedly as he focused intently on the scene before him, an intricate collage composed of every shade of green known to man. The helmet was the worst. Designed to protect him from head injuries, it might well kill him from heat. Many soldiers had modified their helmets to reflect their personalities. Tom had emblazoned 'In Another Land' on his, a psychedelic track from the Rolling Stones that he loved and thought summarized his condition. The humidity, the heat, the altitude all took their toll on the body of a man who had grown up in Chicago.

While it was over ninety degrees with eighty percent humidity where he was, it would have been a freezing New Year's back home. His friends would have been dancing, getting drunk and welcoming in 1968 while he squatted in jungle undergrowth, adrenaline and acute fear playing havoc with his nervous system.

Sleep is elusive in the jungle, and the soldiers had been able to grab it only in fitful snatches. The need to stay alert and the difficulty of negotiating the brutally dense vegetation added to the accumulating fatigue. Tom allowed himself to daydream for a moment. What would his New Year have been like had he been back home? There was a girl he'd met just before he was drafted. Elaine was her name. She was cute and they'd hit it off. They'd been on two dates, had even kissed. What was she doing? Did she even remember him? Was she in the arms of a new boyfriend, sharing a celebratory kiss as the New Year rang in?

A crackle of static shook Tom from his thoughts. He looked behind him to see Ortiz take a message on the radio and pass it up the line. Just then he felt a tree-trunk like arm drop across his shoulders, and he knew it was Eddie Powell, a tall, powerfully built black man who, although he also came from Chicago, had inhabited a very different city. Eddie could have played college football had he gone to college. "Sarge says if we go 500 yards further on this LeRP, we'll be in Cambodia. We need to see if there's anyone in the immediate A-O and not head any further west," his platoon buddy whispered in his ear.

Tom nodded and began to move toward Micky O'Keefe, the man on point, leading the way for the rest of the platoon. O'Keefe had taken a knee and was scanning the barely perceptible path ahead of him, an M16 resting against his body and two belts of ammunition across his chest for the M60 machine gun that Eddie used. While the Americans traveled light in terms of overall equipment, they were heavily armed and looking for a fight.

Tom had taken two steps forward when suddenly, to the left of the track, there was a blur of movement. A Vietnamese man, his face filled with rage, burst forth from his hiding place. His AK47 was aimed at O'Keefe, and the rifle began spewing its powerful 7.62 caliber hail of bullets at the vulnerable soldier, who collapsed to the ground like a puppet whose strings had been cut. Tom had known Mickey for almost the whole tour. His grandfather had been in the trenches of World War I; his father was wounded at Iwo Jima, and now a son of the O'Keefes lay face down in foul-smelling mud on an obscure track in Southeast Asia. Would they think the war was worth his ultimate sacrifice?

As the burst of automatic fire continued, the soldiers threw themselves into the bushes and behind what cover they could find. Someone screamed. Tom brought his rifle to bear only to find the attacker had melted into the undergrowth. The ambush finished as abruptly as it had started.

Tom rushed to O'Keefe and rolled the body over. He recoiled in shock when Mickey snapped open his eyes and coughed and spluttered. Tom, in a state of total confusion, felt around the prone man's body trying to find where he had been hit. Micky yelled out in pain when Tom ran his hands over his chest. "My chest is on fire! It hurts to breathe! Where am I hit, Tom? Am I going to die?"

Tom looked over at O'Keefe's M16 lying on the path and noted the bright silver gashes. Then he saw that the ammo belts on O'Keefe's chest had the same tell-tale marks. Ignoring the panic in Mickey's eyes, he smiled and said, "You are one lucky son of a bitch!" O'Keefe looked confused. "Every round the gook fired hit either the ammo belts or your rifle. Who knew that you could survive being shot at from point-blank range by an AK47!"

"I don't feel lucky," groaned O'Keefe.

"You've probably got a couple of broken ribs," Tom said, ignoring the cries of pain as he hooked his arms under Mickey's armpits and dragged him back to the makeshift perimeter the platoon had hastily improvised. They arrived to the sound of shouts and curses coming from a group of men crowded around something Tom couldn't see. As he drew closer, he saw what turned out to be a pit in the ground. One of the soldiers, a Private Burley, had fallen in during the scramble to find cover. The pit had wooden stakes embedded in its base and, judging by the revolting smell, they had been smeared with excrement. Two spikes jutted through Burley's left leg and one through his right. He was crying and shouting in agony.

Lieutenant Skoberne shook his head. He had just returned from R&R in Sydney, Australia. That precious normality, that comforting familiarity with western life quickly faded as he confronted the primeval hell of Vietnam once again.

Nothing had changed in his absence and now he was back in the shit with everyone else. He motioned to Eddie and Tom. "While you pull out the rest of the stakes, we'll give Burley a shot of morphine. Then you lift him out with the stakes still in his legs."

When Tom looked horrified, Staff Sergeant Zielinski glared at him. "Private Moretti, it's for Burley's own good. We take the stakes out, he bleeds to death, and the wounds are already infected." He indicated their surroundings, "Besides, it's not like we can keep anything sterile out here."

Sergeant Zielinski was a legend in the platoon. He'd signed up at the age of eighteen to fight in Korea; he'd been sent as an observer to see the Brits fighting in Malaya, and now he was on his third tour in-country. Nobody challenged Sergeant Zielinski.

Skoberne shouted to the radio operator, "Call for medevac; we've got two men down."

Tom and Eddie took on the laborious and smelly job they had been given, careful not to touch the injured Burley, who was calming and showing signs of drowsiness brought on by the morphine. Meanwhile, the rest of the platoon began to clear a location suitable for the chopper to land, a job that would take four hours. They used blasting tape to bring down a group of trees and clear a space big enough for a Huey. Were they being watched by the Viet Cong? Probably, but no more attacks came their way. The Americans had lost two men from the field, two fewer Yankees to do the fighting, while the Vietnamese had suffered no casualties. The VC didn't need to push their luck; they had clearly won this encounter.

Burley and O'Keefe made it to the hospital half an hour after the chopper's arrival. Both would be invalided back home. O'Keefe would make a full recovery, but Burley would have his left leg removed from mid-thigh, resulting in a disability that would change the course of his life. The rest of the platoon would spend another night in the jungle, suffering from filth and fatigue and longing for home. Since the latter was a dream away, a hot shower in the safety of their base would do as a compromise.

***

Tom Moretti had never felt so dead inside. Elaine, his wife of nearly fifty years was gone, dead and buried. Breast cancer. It had come on strong and ravaged her body within a year. The love of his life had been broken by the disease and the chemotherapy they had agreed she should undertake to fight it. Now he sat alone in his modest house in Cicero, the crime-ridden Chicago suburb, which, as the neighborhood changed over the years, should have been renamed 'Little Mexico'.

Tom didn't know there could be so many tears or where they could have sprung from. Just when he thought he had no more to shed, a fleeting memory and the still surprising realization that she was gone caught him hard and hit him all over again. Elaine's terminal diagnosis had triggered denial and the first stages of grief even before she died. He simply could not believe that his anchor, the wife who had given him everything he could ever have hoped for, could be dying. It was Elaine who had turned him from a lost veteran into a loving family man. They had done everything together: made a home, brought up a family, shared good friends. What possible reason could there be for her life to be cut short? There had been a terrible mistake. He refused to believe she was really going to die even when he held her hand as she slipped away. This was his experience of the denial stage of grief.

He knew about the five stages of grief – denial, anger, bargaining, depression and acceptance - but discovered they did not work the same for everyone. Anger followed Elaine's death: anger at the doctors for not doing more, anger at God for not saving her, anger at her for leaving him. But mainly he was angry with himself. If love meant anything, he should have been able to do something to save her. Could he have done more? He'd cheated death a few times in his life, but he hadn't been able to help his wife do the same.

The funeral had been a bittersweet affair. It was good to have all the family there, good to have their love and support, but it had been at a price he did not want to pay. The sun had glinted off his wedding ring, the light catching his eye. When he had looked down at the scratched and worn gold band, his thoughts went back to when it had been shiny and new. The memories had released a fresh wave of raw emotions, and Tom had sobbed into the arms of his daughter Sarah, too grief-stricken to care what anyone thought. She had tried to soothe him by saying that everything would be okay. But nothing would ever be okay again. Tom was crushed by overwhelming grief, magnified by his loneliness in a house that had once held boisterous family life. He felt as if he'd been dropped into someone else's story and he didn't know what to do.

The bargaining stage had come to Tom after denial, while Elaine was still alive. If he went to church more often … no, if he went to church and prayed more often … if he gave more to charity … would God let Elaine live? After her death, he went straight from anger to depression, spending too much time in bed, wishing it had been him rather than her. A thick, black cloud followed him wherever he went, just an inch above his head, ready to descend and defeat him at any moment. Acceptance was a long way off; it was simply going to have to wait.

The doorbell rang, forcing Tom from his internal despair. He sighed; he knew what was coming. He put down the lighter he had been fiddling with, ran his hands through his silver-gray hair, smoothed his matching mustache, adjusted his glasses and eased himself out of his armchair to make his way to the front door. It was a familiar ritual he was trying to avoid. He peered through the window to see the mailman with a small package and a fistful of envelopes. He opened the door and received an icy blast of wind for his troubles. The weather was as cold and bleak as his he felt. Tom nodded and wordlessly accepted the post from the outstretched hand of the impatient young Hispanic.

Tom stared down at the envelopes that glared back at him, their bland exteriors camouflaging the pain they would release with the sincere messages inside. It had been a couple of weeks since the funeral but the cards still came. He put them on the hall table and turned his attention to the box, fumbling to open the serious packaging.

Eventually, he resorted to his penknife which opened with a quick snap. The sharp blade made short work of the tape and cardboard. He put the knife away and opened the flaps to reveal a condolence card on top of a box of chocolates. Chocolates. It seemed chocolates were acceptable for a widower; no flowers for him. The strange thing was that Tom had always associated candy with fun and celebrations, so it felt like a fundamental disconnect to receive them now.

Tom tutted as he retrieved the cards from the table and walked back into the living room, putting the box on top of the small stack he had accumulated at the side of his armchair. He sat back in his favorite seat with a grunt and began to work through the bereavement cards, a relentless and miserable process. He knew the messages of support were friends and family reaching out to him, trying to comfort him, but every card was a gut punch of sorrow, screaming at him:

YOUR WIFE IS DEAD   ELAINE IS GONE FOREVER   YOU ARE ALONE OLD MAN

Tears welled up without any warning, and he wept quietly, his head sinking onto his chest. After a while, he rummaged through his trouser pockets and found a handkerchief to blow his nose and dab at his eyes. It was so unfair, after everything he had been through, both in Vietnam and in his job with the Chicago Fire Department. Why was he still alive and his wife, his beautiful Elaine, the first to go? He had always assumed he would be first; it just seemed to be the natural order of things. Didn't women have a longer life expectancy than men? But now she was gone and he was alone in the world. What was left? His children were busy with their own lives, and the grandchildren were turning into adults; nobody needed him anymore. He was just … there, a great big pile of sorrow, taking up space in a world he didn't like or even recognize anymore.

Elaine's passing stirred long-dormant memories of his war in Vietnam. Her death and the feelings of loss brought to the fore painful recollections he had been carefully suppressing for decades. He'd buried them deep; everyday life had dampened them down, but death had brought them back. There was no comfort in the past as the faces of those robbed of their lives reappeared in his mind. It seemed to Tom that his only companions now were the ghosts of the dead. And worst of all was the ghost of the Vietnamese woman. Over the years he had managed to erase her face, but it resurfaced now, ready to haunt him anew. Her eyes, burning bright with tears of unspeakable rage and pain, followed him everywhere. She knew he was to blame and her accusing stare pierced Tom's very soul.

He didn't know how long he had been sitting there, but his stomach rumbled. He checked his wristwatch: 12:27 p.m. He'd missed lunch. He ambled over to the kitchen, pleased to have a distraction. He opened the loaf of white bread and made a baloney sandwich before pouring himself a glass of orange juice. In front of him sat a lazy line of pill pots, which, for a moment, reminded him of soldiers positioned along a dirt track. The orange Perspex containers with white tops and labels had grown in number as he grew in years. The fireman's pension was a good one; his medical bills were covered and a good thing too. It's an expensive business getting old in America.

Tom chewed absentmindedly through the sandwich, forcing the food into his body even though there was a part of him that didn't want it. He washed down his tablets with some of the orange juice and had just sat down again in his armchair when the phone rang. Another sigh, another lurch out of the chair and a brisk walk to the phone to get it before the answering service kicked in.

"Hi, Dad, it's Sarah. I'm just checking in to see how you are."

"Hi, honey, I'm fine," Tom lied. "Been out for a walk this morning. Got some more cards. Really nice messages."

"People just want you to know they're thinking of you, Dad, we all are." There was a pause and a slight intake of breath before she continued, "You know I worry about you being alone in that house; it's too big for you now, too much to take care of. And you need company. Have you thought of getting a dog … or maybe … downsizing?" The dog seemed to be an introduction to a more difficult suggestion. "You could move to one of those complexes for retired people. You know, meet up with folks your age."

Tom sighed; she meant 'old people'. "Oh, well, you know, I'm still trying to figure things out. You're right though; this house is too big for just me, but it would be hard to leave. It's full of memories. I mean, I'm standing in the hallway where you took your first steps all those years ago … and of course, this is where your mother and I spent most of our married lives." He paused as fresh tears filled his eyes. "It's just that, right now, I'm not sure if those memories are a help or a hindrance."

"I know. It's still early days. Everything is still so raw, for all of us."

"I know it's hard for you, too," Tom acknowledged, hoping she would change the subject. He couldn't cope with her grief. It was selfish of him he knew, but he had more than enough pain of his own; he couldn't take on hers as well.

"Look, I'm also phoning to tell you about Easter Sunday. Peter and the family are coming in from Pittsburgh, so I'm getting everyone together. I'll be cooking up a storm, and you have to be there, Dad. It'll be the first time we've all been together since, y'know, the funeral. The kids will keep things lively, and I thought it might be a way to start the healing … for all of us."

Tom smiled. Was that the first one since Elaine died? Sarah had such a big heart, always wanting to make everything right for her loved ones. "Sounds great," he replied, without any enthusiasm.

"Oh, c'mon Dad."

"No, really, it will be good to see everyone. What time do you want me?"

"Any time you want to come. I'll be serving up around noon, but please come earlier. Everybody wants to see you."

"Okay, I'll come early."

"Promise?"

"I promise, honey."

"Okay, bye Dad. Love you."

***

Emily Hawkins stepped out of the nightclub into the cold night air, the blast of music turning into the dull thump of baseline as the club's door closed behind her. Her breath poured out of her mouth like smoke on steroids. Her thick winter coat did the job of warming her body, but her legs only had 10 denier tights to fight off the frosty night - and they were losing. Her short, blonde hair framed a pretty face hiding behind a pair of dark-rimmed glasses. The deeply unfashionable woolen hat her mother had given her was stuffed into her coat pocket.

"Hey, Em, wait for me!" Emily turned around and saw her best friend Jessica moving toward her as fast as she could in her three-inch heels. Jessica's long, dark hair shone in the streetlight; it suited her mixed-race heritage.

"You thought you were going to get away from me, did you?" Jessica asked with a smile. Emily waited for her friend to catch up but didn't respond to the question. "What's the matter?"

"Oh, y'know, it's life, isn't it? Two months ago, Sam said he wasn't that into me, so I lost my boyfriend. Then there was all the family stuff, and now we're just a few months away from finals and then … well, then what? We'll have our degrees and find jobs … and everything will continue along some predetermined path. I worry about the future, but I don't want it to be predictable and boring. I want … oh, to be honest, I don't know what I want."

"So, let me get this right: you're worried about the future because you don't know what you want. Em, we're *all* worried about the future, only we don't talk about it. For most of us, it's the worry of finding a job and starting the lives we've been planning all through school. It's like now we finally have to grow up. That's pretty scary."

Emily smiled at Jessica's unusual earnestness.

"Look, I know you're having a tough time just now," Jessica continued. "Sam's gone but you still have your family - and hello! - I'm still here, like totally. I'll always be here for you, Em. We've known each other since elementary school and became best friends from our first day here at the university, through good times and bad, and the future is not going to change that. Hell, do you remember the time you got so drunk at Karl's party you spent most of the evening chucking up in his toilet? May I remind you again just who kept your hair from falling in?"

"Yep, it was after that I thought it would be a good idea to have my hair cut," Emily laughed as she pointed to her sharp bob.

"Okay, so now I'm unemployed as your party mentor. But seriously, Em, my mom is still friends with some of her childhood buddies, and that was before social media. So, with WhatsApp, Facebook, Instagram and all the other CIA-backed data collection applications out there, we will always be in touch - and under government scrutiny."

Typical Jessica Emily thought, always trying to lighten the mood, but Emily had something else on her mind. "Jess, you know how I've been saving my money from waitressing

"... well, I haven't told anyone, but it's been in the back of my mind that I might take some time out and travel ... y'know, get away and see the world, find out what I can do before I get locked down into doing what's expected." Emily hesitated and then said almost to herself, "... but now that I can go, I'm not sure I want to."

"Oh, my god, Em! You never said anything. I guess I thought, like the rest of us, you'd just look for a job." Jessica paused, wanting to say the right thing. "Travel - what a great idea – but why? Why wouldn't you go if you've been making plans?"

"It's like everything I've done in my life so far has been about getting to the next step up. Y'know, get good grades so you can go to a good university; get a good degree so you can get a good job or go to grad school and get an even better job."

"Don't forget that you're supposed to find a 'good' guy so you can be together forever," Jessica said, trusting Emily to recognize the sarcasm.

But Emily's thoughts had found an outlet and she allowed the floodgates to open. "It's like our lives are all mapped out, and I'm just following a path I never chose. But ... but ... even though I hate the idea of falling into the pattern, I guess I'm really afraid that maybe I'd be better off doing just that. Maybe that's all I'm meant to do, maybe that's all I *can* do."

Jessica caught her mood and responded, "I see where you're going with this. It *is* predictable, isn't it?"

"Predictable and safe and boring. I could jump straight into work and use all my hard-earned savings for the deposit on a rental or put it into a 401K, whatever that is. If I want to travel, I could do what everyone else does and go to Cancun, get wrecked and flash frat boys. But no, I'm going to put everything on hold to go traveling."

"Oh, please tell me you're not going away to 'find yourself'.

Emily replied with a contemptuous snort. "Maybe I've already found myself. Maybe I'm just a twenty-something girl with a nursing degree who knows something about patient care and a lot more about waiting tables in an Applebee's. But no, It's not so much about 'finding myself' as just finding out what I can do, testing myself in another place, one where I have only me to fall back on – see what I'm made of. But the idea is frightening. Maybe I'd be taking on a whole lot more than I can handle."

"Are you kidding me?" Jessica responded tetchily. "Emily Hawkins, you are a smart young woman, brimming with talent and ideas, and you're a lot more than a nursing major who knows the Applebee's dessert menu off by heart. Something made you decide to save up to travel; something in you needs to do this. So go and discover what you can do out there in the world. If you don't, you'll always regret it; you'll always wonder how your life might have been different."

Emily nodded in quiet acknowledgment, a look of determination spreading across her face. "I guess, if I'm going to do this, I should really go for it – no half measures. I've been kicking around the idea of going to Southeast Asia - y'know, Thailand, Malaysia, Vietnam – places that are totally different, immerse myself in completely new cultures. That would be a real test of character."

"Now you're making me jealous, making me wish I could go," Jessica trailed off. "Em, you should do this. Don't think twice. I get that it's a daunting prospect, but you'll never be in a better position to go; there will never be a better time. You're ready, whether you know it or not."

"It means a lot to me that you think so, but please tell me we'll keep in touch while I'm away. I'll probably need a shoulder to cry on."

"Ha! You bet your ass we will. I'll want to know everything that's happening … everything!" Jess said with a wink.

Emily smiled and reached out to hug her friend.

"My Dad is Boston Irish and that's as white as it gets. My mom is from Manila. I have connections to the Celtic music of Ireland and the rice fields of the Philippines, but where's the most exotic place I've been? The 'Pirates of the Caribbean' ride in Disney World."

Emily burst out laughing, her earlier gloomy mood now gone. Jess was the friend she could always count on. Emily knew she would make her trip, and Jessica would be there for her, wherever she was in the world. "C'mon, let's get moving. I'm freezing my ass off and your feet must be killing you."

***

The Hueys descended toward the lush paddy fields with a lurch that threatened to send the contents of Tom's stomach into his mouth. Eddie, sitting opposite, recognized the internal struggle and nodded knowingly. Tom looked sheepish but managed a wan smile. Until the flight to Saigon, he had never flown. Now he'd been in helicopters as well as airplanes, but he still wasn't used to any of it.

There had been a briefing by Captain de Bruin, a good commanding officer and a professional soldier who had joined up before the war. The intel had been of a VC base about a mile into the hills from a tiny hamlet on the edge of Ap Trai Bí, the smallest settlement on the map. The A-O would involve jungle, a likely assault on prepared positions, and then a mountain hike. It was going to be tough and, by the time they hit the trail, Charlie would know they were coming.

The Hueys landed in the designated LZ, their turbines still whirring in anticipation of the briefest of stays. The pilots knew their helicopters were prize targets for Charlie and, while they sat there disgorging their living cargo, they were sitting ducks. The Americans in their drab green uniforms jumped out of the choppers into the knee-deep waters of the paddy fields, while bewildered farmers apprehensively observed the military drama unfolding before them. Soldiers, no matter the uniform, meant trouble. This was not good news for the locals.

There was a roar as the choppers pushed off into the gray sky, their engine noise rapidly dissipating into the sound of angry hornets. The soldiers moved purposefully, fanning out to survey the village. Exposed as they were, they were prime targets for an ambush. Tom could almost feel the crosshairs on him. It was paranoia, but it was justified paranoia. Every footstep forward could be his last if he and the squad came under gunfire. But none came. It seems this village was not an enemy trap.

There was a ripple of panic among the villagers as the troops moved through their huts, searching for weapons, radios or any other telltale signs of VC interaction. Women pulled their children close, and old men scrambled out of the way as the Americans overwhelmed the tiny hamlet. Everyone sensed that the situation could escalate in seconds, and what was a peaceful day could turn quickly into a nightmare of carnage. One young mother caught Tom's eye. He didn't need to understand Vietnamese to see that she feared and loathed them all. She held her baby closer to her breast as Tom's head dropped in an unspoken apology. More than anything, the villagers wanted to be left alone; they didn't care who won the war, they just yearned for the peaceful life that had eluded them for years.

The stores of rice were full, the sign of a good harvest - or were they stockpiled for enemy soldiers? Who knew? The soldiers could have spent more time trying to find something else to corroborate their suspicions, but they needed to keep moving. The crackle of chatter from Ortiz's field radio added an almost robotic feel to the search. They needed to catch the enemy by surprise, get them before they could rally. However, as soon as the men left the village behind, the heavens erupted and Tom was reminded, as if he needed reminding, why the rainforest has its name.

The downpour reduced visibility but also drowned out the sound of their movements; it was 50-50 whether the rain was help or hindrance. All Tom knew was that he was wet to the bone, and he could feel his feet squelching inside his boots as they weaved their way from the village perimeter into dense jungle undergrowth.

Something other than the weather was in the air, all the men sensed it. Something was brewing, and no one needed intelligence briefings to recognize it. Despite Sergeant Zielinski's orders to stop the speculations, it was the talk of the barracks. For about a year now the news had been about the erosion of enemy supplies, men and morale, but try telling that to the marines up near the DMZ who had been pounded for most of '67 by NVA regulars. To the men on the ground, it felt like a spring that had been pushed back, wound and tightened until it had reached its critical point … and then, well … were they about to find out?

Tom scrabbled up the steep edge of the stream. Eddie could see he was struggling and helped him up. Tom nodded his thanks and pulled out his canteen to take a measured gulp. The purification tablets always made the water taste like a chemical cocktail, but at least it stopped him from catching cholera, among other things. It might be raining but the heat was as oppressive as ever, and patrolling through the bush was a sweaty, exhausting affair. Tom couldn't remember the last time his body didn't ache, but he had become accustomed to the sensation of the cotton wool in his head from lack of sleep.

The platoon moved as silently as conditions and equipment allowed as they slogged toward a small hill that had become a base of operations for the VC. Lieutenant Skoberne was talking on the radio as Ortiz scanned the area, his rifle ready to kill any enemy soldiers lurking in anticipation of an ambush. Skoberne tapped Ortiz on the back to signal that he could move on, and the individual squads began to fan out around the base of the hill. If contact with the enemy was made, it was unlikely to be around the perimeter.

Tom began to make his way up the hillside. He was trying to survey his environment for threats while clinging to the gnarled vegetation that stopped him from slipping on the muddy surface. If an enemy soldier appeared on the ridge above him, Tom knew he would be cut down before he could return fire. The briefing had anticipated a firefight and, as usual after contact, a body count would be submitted, Americans and VC. General Westmoreland's idea of the kill count had almost turned combat into a sport: enemy soldiers dead 34, American dead 2. Guess that means it was a win for the U.S., except to the men on the ground it was no contact that felt like a victory.

Tom had no choice but to push on. To his right and left the rest of the men in his platoon slowly clambered up the incline. Everyone counted on everyone else. That was the rule that bound all soldiers together, right or wrong, in jungle or snow, in ancient times or the modern age. The politics were for the old men to worry about, but as a frontline soldier, you covered the guy in front of you or you weren't fit to wear the uniform.

The hill was not very steep or very big, and the Americans quickly got to the nearly flat plateau at the top. This was the last point in a series of ever-increasingly large peaks that ran into Cambodia. It was the leftover, but it was near a village and not too far from a road that led further into South Vietnam. It was a good location for a base of operations: remote but not so remote as to serve no purpose. The G.I.s could see across the hill and began to wave and signal to the men appearing on the other side. They all had made it to the top. But where was the enemy?

Tom could see the camouflaged tops of wooden protection above slit trenches. Had Charlie been home, they surely would have come under withering fire, but there were no silhouettes of gun barrels or men's heads. The place seemed deserted. The Americans crept forward, all weapons trained on the trench line. Tom dropped into the nearest trench where a firing step showed that the VC had fully prepared the position. There was just one thing missing, no VC. Tom looked up toward the backbone of ever greater peaks, concealed now by low cloud. He shuddered. Fighting all the way up those would be a hard slog, a road painted red with the blood of men.

The soldiers moved quickly through the trench works to clear them of the enemy, but no shots rang out. They came to a narrow door leading into what they presumed to be a rabbit's warren of bunkers and subterranean tunnels. In the confined spaces inside, their long M16 rifles would be an encumbrance more than a weapon. Nearest the entrance were the two soldiers with the surname Jones: Moses Jones, who everyone called Mo, was a tall, lean black man who had come straight from the race riots of Detroit to the jungles of Vietnam. Mo had the only shotgun in the group. It was perfect for clearing trenches and tunnels, so he clipped a torch to the front of his shirt and prepared to go in. Robert Jones, who everyone called Alabama, was a pale blonde with a spray of acne across his nineteen-year-old face, the son of a tomato farmer from Dothan, Alabama. He nodded to Lieutenant Skoberne, who gave him his Browning handgun, which became more of a hand cannon in VC tunnels. Alabama also drew his k-bar; the knife was the first weapon of choice in a tunnel. Meanwhile, Zielinski ordered the others to find defensive positions in the trench works, just in case Charlie came home.

The two men went in. The thick earthen walls of the tunnel deadened any noise inside where they found a derelict command center. A few crudely built wooden tables and chairs had been left but nothing else. The slashes of light from their torches roamed the room, throwing shadows at odd angles and highlighting the slick sheen of rain and sweat on their young faces. There were no maps, written communications, ammo or weapons. A few propaganda posters adorned the walls. A burned-out lantern had been stuck into the tunnel earth, but it had long since run out of fuel. Whoever had been here knew the base would be discovered and had left nothing for the enemy.

Mo tapped Alabama on the shoulder and indicated a low tunnel entrance in the corner of the room. The two men crept toward it as Tom peered into the gloom and saw them disappear into a tight black hole. With no sign of any immediate threat, Tom indicated that the rest of the platoon could come into the room to get out of the rain. Mo and Alabama were oblivious to this as they half-crouched, half-crawled their way along the narrow passage,

Mo in the lead. They had switched off their torches; until they were sure they were on their own, there was no point alerting any VC to their location. The heat and humidity forced Mo to squint the sweat from his eyes, each squint making him vulnerable for a split second, but he pushed on. He was beginning to feel claustrophobic, but he shoved the thought from his mind; it was their job to clear the warren of tunnels and make it safe for their brothers-in-arms. He would not, could not, let them down.

Their senses strained in the total darkness. Nothing must give away their position. A stifled cough, a breath or the smell of the body could be enough to betray them – or give them the edge if the enemy faltered. They needed every advantage in a close-quarters' fight. But there was nothing: no noise, no scent, no change of air flow. It felt as if they were in a tomb. Mo made a judgment call and switched on his light. They needed intel as well as a body count.

Mo was about to step into the second room when Alabama grabbed him from behind. "Look down," Alabama virtually breathed into Mo's ear. Mo froze and peered down. His flashlight revealed the ominous dark line of a trip wire. He cautiously stepped over it and saw that the wire was attached to the pin of a Soviet-made anti-personnel grenade. Alabama carefully removed the wire as Mo covered the room. The two anxious soldiers continued the routine of covering each other and squirming into tunnels for another ten minutes until they were satisfied that all the little hideouts and chambers had been discovered. No one was home.

About the same time as Mo and Alabama were reporting back, the rain stopped - just as abruptly as it had started. The men began to mill around the trench work and summit, relief pouring off them like steam from the pools of rain heated by the newly emerging sun. Eddie placed his M60 on the edge of the trench, removed his helmet and produced a pack of cigarettes he had managed to keep dry. "Looks like the dinks ain't home, so smoke 'em if you got 'em," he said with a victorious smile. A few soldiers chuckled, recognizing the easing of tension rather than the comment itself.

Skoberne leaned over and offered his lighter to Eddie, who nodded his thanks. The lighter had the emblem of their division and company on it and had come to be regarded as something of a lucky charm. Many of the men carried one, hoping that an item that had seen them through tight spots would continue to work its magic in tight spots to come. It certainly felt like Skoberne's lighter had worked to protect them today. What could have been a bloodbath had, instead, been little more than an anxious walk in the forest. They'd all felt the strain, but far worse could have happened.

The prepared defensive positions the men had discovered would have been a formidable obstacle to overcome. They would have had to call in either artillery or an airstrike, and the soldiers knew that some of them would have left the hill in body bags. But the abandoned base kept everyone on edge. The overall size indicated a company force of VC had been here. Where were they now? What little evidence they had left showed the site had been evacuated only a short time earlier. Was this force now in the forest around them? Had they infiltrated a nearby village? Or had they used the road to travel incognito into the South Vietnamese interior? The discovery of the hilltop base raised more questions than it answered.

All Tom knew was that he and his friends were unscathed. Nobody died today. It had been a good day, so let the top brass worry about a missing company of men.

***

The American Legion Post on 35th Street in Cicero had been a busy place when Tom came back from Vietnam. For years it served as a haven for the men who returned from the jungles of Southeast Asia only to find themselves the embodiment of a hated establishment. Regarded at best as an embarrassment and, at worst, as pariahs responsible for Agent Orange birth defects, the napalming of civilians and the massacre at My Lai, the men could meet at the legion to share their stories without judgment. But as the years passed, the numbers waned. It is said that time heals all wounds, and Tom was one of the veterans who had moved on with his life, returning only for the occasional reunion or memorial event. The legion itself had had something of a renaissance over the last fifteen years or so as men returned from new wars in far-flung countries, but their homecoming had been very different. 'Support Our Troops' bumper stickers were ubiquitous in the new millennium, the exact antithesis of what Tom had experienced coming back to near civil war in America.

It had been a year or so since Tom had stepped into the utilitarian space of his local legion. He wasn't quite sure why he had come, but the need to visit was like an itch in the back of his mind, an itch he hoped to soothe. A man in a wheelchair sat behind a trestle table, the makeshift reception that nobody had got around to making anything more permanent. The man, in his late thirties, was wearing an immaculately ironed plaid shirt and chinos with the ends of the trousers tucked under him. He had lost both legs above the knee in an IED explosion in Iraq. He had greeted Tom a few times, but Tom couldn't recall the man's name. Their eyes met and the man gave him a smile of recognition.

"Hello there. Tim, isn't it?" the man greeted him warmly.

"Tom, actually, but I'm impressed with your memory. Excuse me, but I don't recall your name."

"It's Rich. How are you doing today, Tom?"

It was a good question. Tom was doing pretty much the same as he had been for weeks: overwhelmed by loss and hopelessness, with a core of pain that made him sick to the stomach. But then he looked at Rich, a man who would have been in the prime of his life had he not been torn into a cripple, just like Burley in the spike-pit, all those years ago. "Not so bad," Tom finally replied. At least he had come home whole, had been able to lead a normal life, able to attract Elaine. What did Rich have going for him? A wheelchair-bound veteran on disability was hardly a good catch. Then he noticed Rich's wedding ring. "You married?"

"Yes, sir, I am."

"How long?"

"Oh, about seven years now. Yep, married with two kids."

Tom was genuinely surprised. "That's good going for a guy …" Tom trailed off. He had no idea how to finish the sentence.

Rich smiled; he'd been in this situation plenty of times. "Listen, when I'm not here at the legion, I'm a radio DJ on the 670 score. I used to play college football, so a returning wounded veteran goes down well with their core demographic. It's a good paying gig." He pointed to his stumps, "And you can do the job sitting down."

Tom smiled to himself. Turns out the guy in the wheelchair had a better life than he had.

"How can I help you?" Rich asked, changing the subject.

"Are any of the old guys here today?"

"Yeah, sure. Lou is running a class and Andy is still the barman."

"Thank you," Tom said and walked down the hall toward the bar area which, over the years, had morphed into part bar, part Starbucks. It didn't feel quite right to Tom, but a new generation of veterans meant new tastes had to be catered for, and it seemed the younger generation was more interested in cappuccinos than Coors.

As Tom approached the bar, Andy spotted him and called out. "Hey, long time no see, buddy."

Tom eased himself onto a bar stool, a room of empty tables behind him. "Beer, please, Andy."

Andy flipped the bottle cap off a Budweiser and put it in front of Tom along with a glass.

"Heard about Elaine," Andy said, matter-of-factly.

"Yeah, it was tough. It's still tough."

"I'm sorry," Andy nodded solemnly.

Tom ignored the glass and concentrated on swigging the beer straight from the bottle. There was silence between the two men until Tom broke it. "Do you ever think about your tour?"

"Sure. Actually, I did two, '68 through to '70. At that point it was better to be in-country than deal with the mess going on back here," Andy said with a hint of pride about the two tours.

"But it was all a lifetime ago," said Tom. "I mean, I spent maybe 2% of my life there, and it all happened half a century ago. Why should that still be in my mind when I can't remember what I had for supper yesterday?"

"It's because it made you who you are. Yesterday's supper is meaningless, but you and me and the other guys around here, we were young men who faced death at a time when we were most alive. Don't think you can see all the scars of war," Andy said, leaning forward.

"We all talk about the war, but for me, the tough times continued afterward, " Tom commented.

"You mean PTSD?" Andy's face now a picture of concern.

"No, well, yes. I had the misfortune to fly back home when there were street riots after King's assassination. I remember, as the plane was coming into Chicago, I could see the smoke plumes. I thought for a minute that the pilot was taking me back to Saigon. I started to panic, thinking there had been some SNAFU with army admin, and I was about to start another damn tour."

"Yeah, I remember that it was only a month later I got my draft papers."

"So, I get home and my mom's treating me like nothing's happened. But I'm different. Dad grasped a little of what was going on in my head. Then I get a message that I'm to report to the nearest military base. They give me a flack jacket and an M16 and send me off with a company of other guys fresh back, and we are no longer walking through the jungles of Southeast Asia but through the streets of our local neighborhoods. I hadn't had time to adjust, nobody had. We were equipped for war, but we were on American soil as crowd control. It was a mess. I remember this guy yelling at us. He had Asian features, almond eyes, and I remember instinctively raising my rifle to take aim because he looked like the enemy I'd been killing for a year. Turns out he was a Japanese college student, but in my mind, his facial features meant 'enemy'. I caught myself, but that kid had no idea how close he came to getting zapped."

There was nothing to say as both men sat thinking about Tom's story. Then he continued, "Somewhere in those stateside patrols, Bobby Kennedy got killed. It felt like I'd brought the violence back home with me ... like what I'd experienced was an infection, and I was the means of carrying it to civilized society."

"It was the worst of times," Andy agreed.

"Ever been back?"

"No, but I would go if I had the money. Why? Are you thinking of going?"

"I don't know. It's just ever since Elaine passed, I'm starting to think about Vietnam again … about all the shit that went down there, stuff I was involved in."

"And you want to know did it mean anything. Hell, you're not the first person to ask that question. We all want that whole goddamn mess to mean something," Andy said, waving his arms around the empty bar to accentuate his point.

"Yeah, but look at the young guys that come here. They came back heroes. And remember our fathers' generation … they won a world war. What did we do? Chase Charlie around the rainforest so we could be labeled 'baby killers' when we came home. No parades for us. We are the generation of soldiers who shamed the nation, the first American army to lose a war. Good men died in those jungles and for what, exactly?"

"Seems to me like losing Elaine has brought a lot of things to the surface. I can't give you the answers; I'm not sure anyone can. You think you want to go back, get some closure, put the past in the past? Then do it, man, and don't delay. None of us is getting any younger."

Tom took another swig from his bottle and looked around. " Tell the truth, Andy, I'm not sure why I'm here or what I was expecting from this visit, but it's been good to talk."

"Anytime, man. Stay strong."

Tom nodded, paid up and made his way back out to the street lost in thought.

***

The house was alive with the noise of family life. Children shrieked and ran around while parents, fighting a losing battle, tried to rein in their youthful exuberance. An eleven-year-old boy flashed past, swinging his lightsabre, a grimacing mother following in his wake, suggesting he continue his game outside. Music was thumping away from an unidentified source, and the TV added to the decibels. Conversation was impossible, not that anyone was trying to have one at the time. Tom sat in the midst of all this and decided, on balance, that he found the hectic atmosphere more agreeable than irritating. He was like the eye of a storm, quiet and still, sitting in a comfy recliner, enjoying a beer and a bowl of potato chips while trying to watch a Cubs' game. This was his family, and he loved them all more than he could say.

"Hey, Dad. Sorry I wasn't here to greet you. Sarah sent me on a beer run," said Peter, Tom's son, as he entered the room and made a beeline to give his father a hearty hug.

"Sounds like your big sister is still bossing you around," Tom said, returning the hug with a smile. "You look good. How's Pittsburgh treating you?"

"Well, I'm the only Cubs' fan in an office of Pirates, but other than that, everything is good. The actuary work is steady. It was the right move."

"Good, glad to hear it. I see Nathan has grown a few inches," Tom said, pointing his beer bottle at the weapon-wielding child who had narrowly missed a vase of flowers with his glowing plastic sword.

Pete nodded and asked, "Was I that loud?"

"You bet your ass you were! And the number of vases and lamps you took out in the early 80s with those damn Star Wars' swords, I figure you owe me 200 bucks in damages."

"Like father, like son, I reckon," Pete conceded. Then, "How are you doing, Dad?"

"Fine, fine," lied Tom. "Your sister is cooking for a small army and it smells good," he added, wanting to keep the conversation light. Sarah was cooking for nearly a dozen people in a house that was normally home to four.

"Everyone get your hands washed; lunch is in five minutes," Sarah called out from the kitchen, her orders accompanied by delicious smells.

There was a flurry of activity as games were brought to a halt, lightsabres were removed to the sounds of protests and trips to the bathroom were made. Finally, everyone was seated at the dining room table. Sarah had been busy and the spread looked delicious: honey-glazed ham with pineapple, sweet potato casserole, green beans with grilled almond slices, spinach salad and cornbread, her mother's recipe. Around the table sat Peter and his wife Claire and their three children: Summer, thirteen; Nathan, eleven and John, eight. Claire was currently acting as a peace negotiator in a simmering war of words between their two boys.

Sarah sat at one end of the table, with her husband David at the opposite end. Their son John, eighteen, was sitting beside his girlfriend Debbie; it was the first time she had met the extended family. Then there was his granddaughter Emily, her last year of university coming to an end. Tom hadn't seen her for a while and wasn't sure he liked her very short, too masculine haircut.

Everyone was hungry and the meal quickly got underway with the clatter of cutlery and the passing of serving dishes. Tom wasn't much in the kitchen apart from toasted cheese sandwiches, which he was pretty sure didn't count. Elaine had seen to that side of things, and now Sarah kept him supplied with homemade meals for his freezer. But eating with the whole family was special, and he was savoring every mouthful. Then, as appetites were satisfied, conversation began to punctuate the sounds of eating.

At first, it all seemed unusually polite and a little superficial, and Tom realized that everyone was tiptoeing around him. The grandchildren obviously had been briefed to be on best behavior, and Summer decided to prove her grown-up credentials by showing an interest in her grandfather's past. "Grandpa, I'm doing a special project in history about the Vietnam War. You fought in that war, didn't you?" Her attempt at a thoughtful question killed the atmosphere more effectively than if she'd lobbed a hand grenade onto the dining room table.

"Summer!" snapped her mother.

"What? It's not about Grandma," Summer said defensively before clamping her hand over her mouth as she realized she had let the cat out of the bag. Both parents winced at her revealing retort.

Tom felt he had to help her out if only to remove the shroud that hung over the room. "Yes, honey, I did. I was there from 1967 to 1968."

"Sick," Nathan nodded approvingly.

"No, Nathan, it was not a good thing. Grandpa came home traumatized by the war, like all the Vietnam veterans, " Summer chided in an attempt to retrieve her own situation while demonstrating her superior knowledge as the older sibling.

"What is traumatized? Is that bad?" Nathan asked his big sister.

"Well, the generals made him drop bombs on villages full of women and children," Summer said, getting into her stride.

"For God's sake, Summer!" Peter dropped his fork in horror at what was coming out of his daughter's mouth.

"What now?" Summer asked defiantly for the second time as tears welled up in her eyes.

Their elder cousin John jumped in, hoping to calm stormy waters and impress his girlfriend at the same time. "Thank you, Summer, but you kids aren't really going to understand the horrors of Vietnam until you see the movies made about the war. But they're all R rated, so you guys need to be a little older before you can watch them."

Tom couldn't help himself. "So, you've seen all the Vietnam movies, have you?"

"Yes, Grandpa, I have and the PBS documentary series, too."

"Great, so which one was the best?"

"For me, it was 'Platoon', the way the men struggle with themselves, let alone the enemy."

"Yeah, well it was a little too clever for me. If we'd spent all that time arguing with the guy next to us, more of us would have died in that damn jungle."

"Well, since you've mentioned 'jungle', Dad," Sarah interjected, desperate to get the family conversation back on track, "Emily has saved up for a trip abroad, and she's planning to start in Vietnam."

Emily looked at her mother in dismay. Why was she being dragged into this car-crash of a conversation?

"Isn't that right, honey?" Sarah added, looking at Emily expectantly.

"Er, yeah, I uh, I've been saving all my tips, and I'm going to fly out right after I finish my finals. I'm going to start in Ho Chi Minh City."

"Yeah, I remember it when it was Saigon," Tom said a little too gruffly.

"I guess I'm following in my grandfather's footsteps," Emily added weakly.

"It's funny you should say that because I've been thinking about going back and revisiting some of the places I can remember ..." Tom struggled to find the right words, " ... when I served in Vietnam."

"Dad, that's great!" Sarah enthused, seizing an unexpected opportunity. "And you know what? I think this is a chance to kill two birds with one stone. David and I are very worried about our little girl going off to the other side of the world, all by herself, isn't that right?" Sarah asked, now looking for unequivocal support from her husband.

"That's right," David said, wisely choosing the path of least resistance.

"And if you were to go to Vietnam on your own, Dad, I would be twice as worried ... so why not go together?"

"Mom!" Emily blurted out in sheer disbelief, all her plans shattered in one sentence.

Tom looked at his granddaughter who was now staring studiously at her plate, her cheeks aflame. If Sarah had a flaw, it was her overprotectiveness. She fretted about her kids' happiness, her husband's workload and her parent's well-being. That heart of hers again. Sometimes it was overwhelming, but the thought of his naïve young granddaughter with a boy's haircut finding her way around the bustling streets of a foreign city made Tom uncomfortable, too.

"Emily, you've never been out of the states and, while my memories of the country are older than your mother, I assure you, you've no idea what you're walking into. So, personally, I would feel more comfortable if we went together. You can see the sights, and I can do what I need to do."

Emily could only hear the pounding of her heart in her ears. Months of saving and planning had been destroyed by her mother in that one throwaway remark. Or was it a throwaway remark? Had this whole thing been a set-up to make sure they went together? Emily hadn't a clue, but her mother had no right to interfere without consulting her. She loved her grandfather, but what twenty-one-year-old woman would want to take theirs on the trip of a lifetime? It was utterly unfair, but what could she do? She was completely and comprehensively trapped. Everyone at the table was staring at her, waiting to see what she would say.

She looked up and met her grandfather's eyes, her vision blurred by tears. "It would be my pleasure, Grandpa."

***

The men of the platoon marched back into camp, tossing their detritus into the fires of the constantly lit oil drums as they passed by them. Specialist Ramirez from another squad in the platoon got there first and took out C-ration wrappers and cigarette butts, his m79 grenade launcher slung casually over his shoulder. Eddie dropped in some gum wrappers and two empty cigarette packs.

Mo was lecturing Alabama on how the black man was fighting the white man's war. Alabama looking confused. "But I'm a white man and I didn't want to fight in Vietnam." Mo was about to apprise Alabama of his own views when Zielinski glowered at him. The private immediately shut up and started to take an immense interest in the contents of his pockets, which he began chucking into the fire.

Zielinski's thoughts were interrupted as he approached the oil drum and heard Ortiz say, "Sergeant, Lieutenant Skoberne asked to have a debrief after chow."

Zielinski threw in some damp notes, now smudged and redundant, and the remains of his blasting tape. "Affirmative, Ortiz. You go get some hot food in you, too."

Men were still dumping their debris into the oil drums when it dawned on Zielinski that he'd just thrown high explosives into a fire. He had seconds to retrieve them or be responsible for killing the very men under his command. Without hesitation, he jammed his hand into the flames and, crying out in pain as his skin was seared by the fire, he clamped onto the tape, whipped it out and hurled it away from the blaze. It all happened so fast that the men around the oil drum weren't quite sure what their sergeant had done.

"Medic!" Eddie cried out as he stared at Zielinski's blistering skin. Zielinski was led away by Doc McCarrick, the company doctor, as the men began to piece together the chain of events that had led to their best NCO being hospitalized.

It was all the men could talk about in the mess tent, but later, back in their bunks, they found less serious topics of conversation. Eddie sat down and lit up. Tom glanced over to see if he was smoking a joint; with Zielinski gone, it might be worth the risk. Eddie read his mind and said quietly, "I thought about it but it seems kinda disrespectful

– like I'd be doin' something behind his back and it wouldn't be fair … under the circumstances." Tom nodded his understanding and watched as Eddie leaned over and dropped the needle on his Otis Redding & Carla Thomas album. The snap and crack of 'Tramp' became the backdrop to their conversations.

"Shit, Eddie, this soul stuff again? When are you going to play some real music, like Johnny Cash or Jack Greene?"

"When I have my ears cut off? " Eddie replied with a raised eyebrow.

Tom and Mo laughed.

"That's no laughing matter," chided Ortiz. "Charlie's been known to cut the ears off of dead G.I.s."

"Yeah, well, there's that crazy guy Humford in B Company. He's been collecting ears off gooks for a while," Mo announced as the levity of seconds ago evaporated.

"Humby," Tom corrected.

"What?" asked Mo.

"The private's name is Humby."

Mo put his hands on his hips and cocked his head to one side. "Honky, I am talking about a man who collects human ears, and you want to correct me on his name?"

"Sorry, Mo, you're right. I've seen the necklace and, sweet Jesus, what is this place doing to us that a guy from America, the most civilized country in the world, turns into some kind of mindless savage? That is one bad dude," Tom observed.

"Hey, guys, knock it off. I'm trying to listen to the soothing sounds of soul music, except my ears are being filled with stories about savages and shit," Eddie growled, throwing his canteen of water playfully at Mo.

Mo didn't see the canteen coming, and it clanged against the side of his head. He let out a yelp of pain and surprise, and everyone roared with laughter. Mo rubbed the side of his head and scowled at Eddie.

"Hey, if that canteen is the only friendly fire we've taken recently, that's fine by me."

"And at least nobody got zapped out there in the village or tunnels," Ortiz added, which elicited the sounds of agreement.

Mo brought the banter back to his canteen-related injury. "Hey, Eddie, us brothers got to stick together; conscription is the same as slavery."

"Say what?" Eddie retorted.

"The white man is brutalizing the black man back home. Nothing has changed in a hundred years."

"Wasn't it the ni ..." Alabama stopped when he caught both Mo and Eddie scowling. "I, ah, mean the blacks, who attacked the police in Detroit?"

"Nah, man, they started shooting looters, and then they just started shooting anybody. Hell, they even killed three innocent brothers in a motel room. For what? Booking a motel room with intent to sleep?"

Alabama looked cowed.

"So, it seems if you're a poor black man, you get to be unemployed or a police target or you get your ass drafted over here."

"Actually, I joined up all by myself," Eddie replied.

"Now why would you want to do something stupid like that?" Mo sneered.

"Because my daddy served in a tank crew in WWII. He was proud of his service, and I wanted to make him proud of me. Besides, regular pay and meals, I thought it seemed like a fair deal."

"That's exactly why I joined up, too," Alabama added.

"Guilty," Ortiz said, raising his hand. "My parents said it was God's work fighting these atheist communists."

Tom smiled. "I guess you and me, Mo, are the only conscripts here. Does that make me an oppressed black man, too?"

The others couldn't help but laugh. Reality had taken the wind out of Mo's sails, but he wasn't to be deterred. He turned back to Eddie, saying, "Brother, you and me, we need to be a unified force against this southern white trash." He said this while hooking a thumb at Alabama.

"Who you callin' 'southern white trash'?" Alabama asked defiantly.

"Easy, Alabama, you are the very definition of southern white trash," Tom said with a cheeky smile.

Alabama shrugged to yet more laughter from the tent. The soldiers were almost manic in their attempts to amuse and distract each other. The constant patrols, minor firefights and the ever-present threat of danger meant that rest time back in camp was all about forgetting a reality that included the very real possibility of their imminent demise.

Most of the men had smoked before, tobacco mainly, but now everyone smoked as much as possible if only because it kept the bugs away. Some indulged a new-found taste for the best marijuana money could buy. The Vietnamese produced high-quality weed at cheap prices, but frontline officers strictly enforced the ban on drugs. They particularly hated marijuana because it made the men dopey and docile, qualities they did not want in combat troops. Whatever they smoked, the men knew it was bad for their health, but that threat was long-term. All that mattered now was today, just get through today.

Alabama didn't read the local newspaper from his hometown anymore; his reading wasn't that great anyway. He didn't care how college football was doing; what the hell did it matter? In any fight that was kill or be killed, Alabama planned on taking down as many of those dink bastards as he could - before they got him.

Eddie had arrived with a pocket diary to mark off the days, at least that's what he had done for the first four months. Now he didn't bother. What was the point if he was going to be dead before the end of his tour?

Ortiz had always been religious. He remembered the pride in his parents' eyes when he had become an altar boy, but that was years ago in a time of innocence. Vietnam had sucked his faith right out of him. How could God – any god - allow the violence and brutality perpetrated by all sides? Every village they walked into was full of terrified locals, scared because of what they were hiding or scared because they had been threatened by the VC or scared because they had heard stories about American atrocities and scared because their village might be the scene of the next crime. Agent Orange, napalm, B-52s, Claymore mines. The military industrial complex knew no limits to destruction and seemed oblivious to the fact that their weapons radicalized the population more effectively than communist ideology . The politicians in Washington never figured out that killing thousands of Viet Cong would not result in success unless the politicians of South Vietnam had the support of the locals, something they never had.

Ortiz's biggest fear was exhausting the radio batteries, but that became a risk only for deep-penetration patrols when they'd been out for a week or more. So far his squad had missed that. Secretly, in his most private thoughts, he acknowledged that the violence made him feel powerful. Using just his voice to call for artillery or airstrikes was exhilarating. He was a mere mortal causing fire from the sky to rain down on those who sought to harm him and his brothers. That ability, that authority unleashed the primitive and intoxicated him. His faith had been replaced with a feeling of ethereal power from the receiver of his radio. He wondered if it was a fair trade - to be damned, but powerful.

When it came to religion, Mo had gone the other way from Ortiz. As a kid, he had attended church on Sundays because that's what the family did, but he'd never thought much about it, never questioned if he had the faith to support his actions. That was the case until the summer of '67 and the brutal crackdown on the Detroit ghetto, when real soldiers from the 83rd and 101st Airborne divisions were on the streets of an American city. Americans died fighting Americans. As the police and the National Guard fired on houses, he started praying not only for his life, but also for the lives of his black brothers and sisters. Now, when bullets buzzed past his head in the jungle, when mortar rounds exploded close enough to send the shock wave reverberating through his chest, he believed his prayers had been answered, that it was Jesus who had heard him and saved him. He'd never been good at reading, but he had traded a pocket knife for a pocket Bible back in Detroit, and the treasured book, carefully wrapped in plastic for protection, had come to war with him. It comforted Mo to flick through it, to pick out meaningful words as he tried to glean any information about what the good Lord had in store for him.

Tom didn't write home anymore. His father, who had served with distinction in North Africa and Italy in World War II, always wanted to know what the fighting was like in America's new war. Tom couldn't lie, but he didn't have the heart to tell him.

***

Tom was breathing heavily and paused before ringing the bell. A young black woman answered the door and smiled when she saw him.

"Hello, Kiara. You need to do something about those steps. I swear they're getting steeper," Tom mock-complained, returning her smile. "Is he in?"

"Well, where else would he be?" she asked in their time-honored exchange.

Tom knew his way to the front room of a house that had seen better days. He also knew that's where he would find Eddie, sitting in the same strategically placed armchair for the best view of the TV. His old friend was now a virtual skeleton of a man, a shadow of his former self, but he looked the same as he always did on these visits, with his oxygen mask in place and some sparse gray curls doing their best to cling to the side of his head. Skin hung off his bones the way the over-large cardigan hung off his once great frame. Every breath he took was accompanied by gentle wheezing in his fight against the emphysema that ravaged his lungs. His rheumy eyes, framed by thick glasses, sparked to life when he saw his old pal. "Tom … how are … you?" rasped Eddie between thin lungfuls of oxygen.

Tom looked down at the wasted body of his once formidable friend. Sometimes it seemed age and illness were crueler than any fate they could have suffered in Vietnam. "Better than you," Tom said with a wry smile.

Eddie began to laugh, but the laugh rapidly turned into a hacking cough, followed by a bout of wheezing as he got his breathing under control again.

"Sorry, Eddie," Tom said, horrified at how a simple joke looked as though it could have been the end his oldest friend.

Eddie waved away the apology. A visit from Tom was the highlight of any day. Half alive, half dead, his family tip-toed around him like he was a ghost, something to be feared and pitied at the same time. But Tom was always the same. Maybe he was gray and wrinkled on the outside, but inside he was the same man Eddie had always known. At least, that had been true until the death of Elaine. Now Tom and Eddie made the perfect pair: Eddie had the broken body and Tom, the broken soul.

"I'm going back to 'Nam," Tom announced.

"Can I … come too? … I just need … to get my boots," Eddie said dryly and then asked, "Are you … serious?"

"Yes."

"Why now? … Why all … of a sudden?"

"I don't know exactly. Elaine's passing has dredged up all kinds of memories, a lot of them about our time in 'Nam. I guess I need that closure everyone talks about. And there's this," Tom said, producing a lighter from his pocket.

"Finally going … to do it … huh?" Eddie wheezed.

"I've carried it all these years, but now it's nagging at me," Tom said, nodding at the lighter. "I keep turning it over in my head … what were we doing there? What was all the fighting about? Why all the bloodshed over a stupid mountain trail? Was anything worth all that death?"

"You've been struggling … with that … since we got back," Eddie coughed.

"What do you mean?"

"Did it ever … occur to you … why you … became a fireman?"

"Good pay, no college needed; it was local."

"That could be … a lot of jobs … No, you chose it … because it was your way … to make amends …   It was your way … to save more lives … than you took."

Eddie's comment floored him. All these years, all this time, and it had never dawned on him that this was the reason he was drawn to his work. He had subconsciously chosen a career about saving lives, a way of compensating for those he had taken. Eddie was right. "Aren't you the great philosopher," Tom said, looking at Eddie with new eyes.

Eddie put his thumb up in agreement.

"The woman's come back, too." The two of them had often discussed the ghosts they'd brought back with them.

"We did … what we were told … what we had to do …"

"Never made it right though."

"And you want … to go now … because your anchor … to the present is gone … All you have left … is the past."

"Become psychic recently?" Tom asked, surprised again at Eddie's level of insight.

Eddie shrugged. "If something's ... telling you to go ... you need to go ... I hope you get ... the closure you're ... looking for."

Tom hadn't realized until then that he needed Eddie's approval for the trip. Some might have said that it was a foolish idea, a journey that would only stir painful memories, but Eddie was on the same wavelength. Tom had what he needed, but he stayed on to chat and share a bowl of pretzels while they drank Cokes and watched 'Jeopardy'.

***

Emily sat in the coffee shop with Jessica, blinking back tears.

"So, let me get this right," Jessica said, her mind still reeling from the flurry of information her friend had just downloaded. "Your trip of a lifetime has just been hijacked by your grandfather. He's going to head out to Vietnam with you and ... what, exactly? You guys are going to be, like, drinking buddies?"

"Yes!" exploded Emily. "That's about the size of it."

Silence descended. Emily sniffed and stirred her latte. "I mean, I love my grandpa, I really do. One of my earliest memories was visiting him down at the fire station and sitting in one of the engines with a way-too-big-and-heavy fire helmet on my head, my little hands clutching the wheel and my smiling grandpa sitting beside me. I was so proud to be his granddaughter. He made me feel like I could be a fireman too. I was excited and proud and happy, but I'm not six anymore, am I?"

"No, you're not and, while we all love our grandparents, it doesn't mean that as adults we should go on holidays together. Is there no way you can get out of this?"

"Sure, if I want to incur the wrath of my mother and break my grandfather's heart. Would you pay that price?"

"Hey, my only living grandparent is my Boston Irish grandma, and she's usually in a drunken stupor by 11 a.m. She loves her Jamesons, " Jessica said with a shrug. "Look, he was there before, and he's combat trained; he could be useful in a tight spot."

"You must be joking. The last time he was there he was young and fit and busy getting shot at. He's in his seventies now, having spent his entire adult life in Cicero. Jesus, he couldn't hurt a fly."

"Hey, take it easy. I'm just trying to find a silver lining here," Jessica replied, stunned by the strength of Emily's response.

"And you know what the worst thing is?" Emily added, flicking her wooden stirrer so that it landed across the table.

Jessica was starting to tire of this conversation. This was not the end of the world. She felt for her friend, but really, there would be life beyond this one trip. "No, what?"

"It's the fact that," Emily began, not spotting her friend's declining interest, "to save money, we're going to share a double room."

This new information renewed Jessica's interest in the conversation.

"I mean, he's old. What if the heat gets to him, or he has a heart attack - or worse? I don't want to be responsible for something happening to him. I don't want to be the one who has to tell Mom that Grandpa's dead."

"My dear Emily, you haven't thought about the bigger picture," Jessica said with a mischevious smile.

"Dead isn't the big picture?"

"No, because you're going to have to endure something that nobody but you will care about."

"What?" Emily asked, her eyes wide in anticipation. What had she overlooked?

"You are going to see your grandfather coming out of the shower all wet and saggy, with just a towel wrapped around him."

"Oh, sweet Jesus, I hadn't thought of that." Emily allowed the revolting image to enter her head and shuddered. "But bad as that is, I thought you were going to say something else ... something about the fact that I wouldn't be able to ... ummm ... entertain anyone else in the room. Nothing like that is gonna happen with Grandpa for a roommate."

"Are you hoping to meet someone?"

"Maybe. You never know. I'm open to the possibility, and some fit male company *would* be nice."

"You mean someone like Eric?"

"Well … he *is* a good reason to take self-defense classes. And the bonus is that I'm developing my arms and upper body strength. I am gonna look so hot this summer! But If all six foot, two inches and 180 pounds of Eric weren't demonstrating the moves, I would *not* be a regular."

"Hey, no fair! I was the one who got you to go in the first place. I was the one who told you about Eric 'buns of steel' Rochester."

"You snooze, you lose," Emily winked as she finished off the dregs of her latte, got up and grabbed her gym bag. "Let's get to the gym so I can forget about this conversation for an hour at least."

Jessica followed her lead as they headed off to see who could flirt more outrageously with the unsuspecting Eric. What neither of them knew was that Eric had kept his homosexuality secret so he could join the marines and serve with distinction in Afghanistan.

***

Eddie shook Tom from a deep sleep, saying, "C'mon, man, wake up! Ortiz has tuned the radio into something. Whatever it is, it's big and it's real bad."

A groggy Tom blinked away his sleep, hurriedly put on his boots and grabbed his rifle and helmet to follow Eddie to the tent where virtually all of the platoon huddled around the field radio. Ortiz sat in pride of place, acting like the conductor of the disaster that was unfolding.

"… ICTZ reporting heavy fighting in Huế, both in and around the city. ARVN troops responding …" crackled the radio.

Tom was still slow to understand what was going on. "Aren't we in the middle of a cease-fire for Tet? Hasn't there been a general agreement that nobody would be fighting around Huế? It's, like, sacred to the gooks or something, isn't it?" Tom asked his questions in an attempt to make sense of a situation that made no sense, but judging by the looks on the rest of the men's faces, they were just as bewildered as he was.

"Oh, it's everywhere, man," Alabama tried to explain. "It's SNAFU. Them dinks are hitting everywhere, even Khe Sahn."

"Khe Sahn is always getting hit. Those poor bastard marines, I doubt they've had a day without someone getting zapped," Ortiz corrected, then shushed the group as more news was coming in.

"… company strength enemy units assaulting My Tho and Ben Tre. Local ARVN forces being pushed back … marines and naval personnel responding."

"Aren't those places down south in the Mekong Delta?" Tom queried. What he was hearing baffled him even more. Was the whole country about to fall to the communists?

"Alabama is right," explained Eddie." It's happening all over the country. Must be at least a dozen key places being fought over now. There is even fighting in Saigon." As if to confirm this, an update reported an attack on the national radio station.

"Who's winning that one?" Mo shouted out.

"Only one way to find out," Ortiz responded. The whole country was seemingly collapsing to the commies, but it was all playing out through his radio. In front of him was a captive audience, an audience that listened to what he alone could provide. A feeling of power surged through him; he was the DJ from hell. With a little flourish, he re-tuned the radio to the national news station. As soon as he did so, 'Hello, Goodbye' by the Beatles blared out, and there was a huge cheer from all the soldiers.

"Wait!" urged Mo. "We don't know if that means our guys or the gooks have the station."

"Oh, c'mon. The Beatles are hardly on Charlie's hit parade. I've never been so happy to hear white people music in all my life," Eddie retorted.

"I did not expect to hear the latest Beatles' record this way," Alabama remarked, more to himself than anyone else.

The men listened to the end of the song. No matter who they were or what their musical tastes, they all smiled as they tapped their feet to the beat of the jaunty tune that seemed to be an almost light-hearted military plan for a counter-attack. "I don't know why you say goodbye, I say hello ..."

Like any good DJ, Ortiz waited for the song to end and then went back to the serious news. The mood of the room was at his command. Every man here thought the gun was the most powerful weapon on the battlefield, but Ortiz knew the truth: it was the radio. The communications that came over could mean the difference between life and death for everyone. He turned the dial back to military frequencies.
"... I say again, the U.S. Embassy compound is under attack. All local units to respond immediately. The perimeter wall has been breached. Enemy commando units are inside the compound."

"No fucking way!" Tom summarised what everyone was thinking. The attack on the American embassy felt like an attack on America itself. It was the most heavily guarded compound in the whole country, maybe the whole world. If that wasn't safe, then where was? Virtually all the fighting had been in the jungles, hills and countryside. Huế and Saigon had not been the focal points of any previous fighting, and yet these so-far unscathed cities, packed with civilians, were now in the crossfires of war.

"Hasn't Saigon only got ARVN and MPs in the area?" Ortiz asked.

"Well it's about damn time those assholes got a taste of what it's really like in-country," growled Eddie.

"Particularly the MPs. All they do is harass the real soldiers who are just blowin' off steam in the bars," Ortiz agreed.

"Hey, Ortiz, ain't you the one always following behind the rest of us? You're like those MPs for our squad," Alabama joked.

"Hey, screw you, farm boy! Do you want to carry that radio pack in the ninety-degree heat, the sweat pouring off you because of the humidity?"

At that moment Lieutenant Skoberne stepped into the tent. Fresh from an officers' briefing with Captain de Bruin, he registered the alarm and confusion on the faces of the men staring at him. He was the platoon's officer but, right now, he wanted to be a private, to have the certainty that the officers above him knew what they were doing. They were all expecting answers, but with the entire intelligence structure in disarray, there were none, at least not yet. Everything they knew had been turned on its head. Everything Westmoreland and the President had been saying was wrong, and the proof was in the sounds of mortar rounds and automatic gunfire in the ancient city of Huế and the capital city of Saigon.

The men stood to attention, the radio continuing to blare out the news of the chaos that was engulfing all of South Vietnam. "What news, sir?" Corporal Ventura asked.

Skoberne breathed deeply and stifled a sigh. He had a choice: he could do what the senior officers wanted, or he could do what his men needed. He opted for the latter. "As you were. Men, I'm not going to lie to you; it's a mess out there. General Westmoreland seems to think that all these attacks, from the Mekong Delta in the south, through the capital, up to the DMZ, are diversions so the enemy can overrun Khe Sahn."

"That's bullshit!" Mo blurted out and instantly regretted it. Had Sergeant Zielinski been there, he would have been put in the brig for a week for his insolence. "Sir, very sorry about that outburst, sir," Mo said sheepishly.

"Under the circumstances, I'll let it slide because ..." Skoberne paused. What he was about to do would break every conceivable army regulation, but today felt like a good day to do it. "... because I happen to agree with you, and I think that in twenty-four to forty-eight hours, so will the general. It appears that under the guise of the ceasefire, Charlie has infiltrated all the major urban locations across the south and coordinated simultaneous attacks to take place today, just as local ARVN units are going home for the holidays."

None of the G.I.s, Tom included, had ever been impressed by the ARVN fighting capability. Most of them felt like they were doing all the hard work while the South Vietnamese soldiers cruised along on their efforts. Tom raised his hand.

"Yes, Private Moretti."

"Excuse me, sir, but isn't this a good thing ... in a way?" There was a general murmur at the stupidity of what Tom had just said.

"Silence men, let the private speak."

"Thank you, sir. What I mean is that although this attack did catch us with our pants down, hasn't the problem always been trying to find significant numbers of the enemy in the bush? I mean, haven't we been years humping up hills, wading across rivers and hacking through jungles, trying to find enemy squads? Now we know where they are. There must be thousands of those commie bastards fighting in populated urban areas where they can't hide spike-pits or disappear into the bush. We've got them, haven't we, sir? Isn't it time to lock and load and kill those dink bastards where they stand?"

There was a roar of approval from the mass of men in front of Skoberne. He allowed a smile to creep across his face. War was the ultimate dichotomy; it brought out the very worst and also the very best in people. These young men, many too young to legally drink, were willing to take the fight to the enemy. He didn't smell fear or defeat, but anger and savagery.

"Moretti's right. And I think that within twenty-four hours we are going to be sent to one of these sites to kill us some commies," Skoberne said with a smile.

The men of the platoon stamped and cheered. The electricity in the air was the tension men feel just before a hunt. Their blood was up, and their resolve was fire in their veins. You could smell it. The soldiers were no longer men; they were hounds baying for blood. The scent of the quarry filled their nostrils, and they were now in a state of bloodlust, yearning for violence and demanding death.

Skoberne had watched the mood change from bewilderment to anger and then to something darker, something animalistic. He decided to indulge the bloodlust; it was something that could be harnessed. He ordered the men to prepare to move quickly, all kit packed, radio batteries charged, guns cleaned, k-bars sharpened, extra ammo stashed. It was time to go to war.

***

Emily gently shook Tom from a deep sleep, saying, "We've just landed, Grandpa," a look of concern on her face.

A groggy Tom blinked away his sleep, rubbed his eyes, put on his glasses and reached for his Cubs' baseball cap. He hadn't known if he could sleep on the flight, but it turned out he was a natural. His joints were stiff, part airplane seat, part age, but he grabbed his bag from the overhead locker and followed his granddaughter as they filtered out of the 747. Then there was passport control and baggage pickup, rituals that most of the passengers knew well but were new experiences for Tom. He was impressed with Emily's effortless handling of the procedures. She was young and vulnerable but not afraid to strike out on her own. He was proud of her.

Once out of the arrivals hall, they entered the main airport to look for the way to the taxi rank. Tom was stunned. There had been a roughly 50/50 split between Vietnamese people and Americans of various ethnicities on the plane, but now he was in a sea of almond eyes and black hair, a sea of perpetual motion. Smatterings of an alien language filled his ears. He remembered the odd word. *Chào anh* was some variant of hello. He had heard it often enough during his tour to realize he was never going to be able to learn the language.

The sounds brought everything back. Tom could feel himself break out in a sweat. Was it the heat of the night or the panic in his heart? Charlie was everywhere. Any one of these men could step out in front of him, pull out a Browning pistol and blow his Yankee ass away. But that was stupid, that was fifty years ago.

It was late but everywhere was noisy and hectic, the nighttime lights casting eerie shadows on the sidewalk. Emily saw the panic in her grandfather's eyes and took his hand, a loving gesture that touched him as she confidently guided them toward the taxi rank. The role reversal from times gone by did not escape him.

Tom noticed that fashions had changed, which was hardly surprising. A few older people, both men and women, still wore the traditional tunic over trousers, but far more wore

colorful t-shirts, shorts and jeans, although to him, jeans looked too hot for the stifling heat and humidity. He was wearing a blue polo shirt and khaki Dockers; Emily was wearing L.L. Bean tropical trekking pants and a tight white t-shirt, which she had chosen to show off her toned arms and torso. But whatever they wore, they were not going to blend into this crowd.

As they made their way, they were hassled by a few street traders using broken English to sell their wares, but Tom stepped in front of Emily to protect her and remembered,

"*Không nhờ*". The traders looked surprised that a westerner knew any Vietnamese and moved on. When they finally secured a taxi, they put their cases in the trunk and were off to their downtown hotel. The streets had some bicycles, a few trucks, the occasional car and hundreds of motor scooters, which were obviously the Vietnamese vehicle of choice. Tom smiled when he saw a husband and wife seated on their small two-stroke engined scooter, a toddler on the father's lap, her hands on the handlebars, mimicking the driver. The mother had a baby strapped to her chest. A whole family on a two-seater scooter.

After the incessant noise of the traffic and the general hubbub of the streets, Tom and Emily were relieved to get to the hotel. They made their way up to the assigned room and dropped onto their beds, where Tom had a fitful night's sleep before starting their first day in Vietnam.

***

Long Nguyen sighed as he lay in bed, his middle-aged body showing the first faint resistance to his will, the revelations of aging starting to creep up on him. This was it, the three minutes of groggy bliss between sleep and reality, that all-too-short period of languor before full consciousness. Family life was about to destroy this brief bit of zen-like calm.

When he had first met his wife, some twenty years ago, they were both students at the Vietnam National University. Chau, her name meant pearl, matched her name. She was all coy looks and well-bred conversation, but that soon changed. As their romance blossomed, they became intimate, first with each other's thoughts and, later, with each other's bodies.

And then there was married life. Long knew that as an engineer, he had a naturally mathematical mind, and he couldn't help but track the inverse correlation between sex and nagging in a relationship. In the beginning, there were no complaints and a lot of sex; nowadays the reverse was true. The presence of three children, all under the age of ten, hardly made for romantic opportunities, but surely there must be times when his wife could stop being a mother or career coach and remember to be a lover. He understood that the children took up most of her time and energy, but unlike Chau, Long didn't define himself through his children's lives. Perhaps that was the fundamental difference between a mother and a father.

Long's career was the bane of Chau's life, and she had made it her mission to berate him for not getting the promotions he deserved. It was complicated, and she knew it, but she chaffed under the realization that he was better than his job, much better. A promotion would mean more money, and more money would mean that they could move to a better part of the city or, at least, get out of this two-bedroom apartment that slept five.

"Breakfast," came the call to action from Chau.

That was it, time's up. It was the signal for Long's three-year-old daughter Ahn to wander in and insist that daddy was getting up and going to work. She was adorable, that was true, but he would have preferred another fifteen minutes of sleep. Long shut his eyes and breathed heavily, pretending to be sound asleep. He could hear the padding of little feet getting closer to him, followed by a silent pause while Ahn considered what to do to wake her father.

Long felt a little finger poke him in the arm, but he didn't move. Another pause as his daughter thought about her next move. Then Long felt a pair of dribbly lips push up against his ear, and Ahn shouted as loudly as she could, "Wake up, Daddy!" His game had backfired spectacularly. Long winced and snapped his eyes open, letting out a roar, while he grabbed Ahn and hoisted her up to him for a quick hug. She let out an excited squeal as he nuzzled her plump cheeks.

"Breakfast time, Daddy," she announced, very pleased with herself.

Long nodded and let Ahn run off to find her mother. With a herculean effort, he hoisted himself out of bed and, resplendent in his white vest and underpants, wandered to the kitchen to find a bowl of *pho* waiting for him. One benefit of having a mother for a wife was that the cooking was excellent, and he eagerly gobbled up the spicy noodles. He loved the fact that Chau made it hot enough so that he didn't have to add any chili.

"Are you going to talk to your manager about another job today?" Chau asked.

Long sighed. By 'another job', Chau meant that he needed to raise the possibility of a promotion.

"Not today, now's not the right time."

"Well, when *is* the right time?"

Long caught himself before he sighed again. At this rate, he would suck out all of the oxygen from the apartment, and he did want his family to live, most days anyway. Instead, he chose to ignore the follow-up question and tried a casual approach to tell Chau some news she wasn't going to like.

"I'm going to leave early and walk my mother to Tao Dan Park before my shift starts. She does so love to sit and watch the world go by, and you know how frail she is. I promised her I'd come by this morning."

"But it's your turn to take the boys to school," Chau said, putting her hands on her hips, an early warning sign of a potential fight. Long had to think fast and knew that by offering her what she wanted, he could get what he wanted.

"I'm planning to hang back after my shift and talk to the director. He's coming for an inspection today," he said in what he hoped was a nonchalant way.

"I thought you said it was not the right time," Chau said suspiciously.

"It isn't, with my boss. He's preoccupied with the director's review, but the visit will give me an opportunity to speak to the director personally. I wanted to keep it a surprise, but there you go, you got it out of me."

Chau's face lit up.

Operation Keep Mother and Wife Happy accomplished thought Long and congratulated himself on his brilliant handling of a tricky situation. He quickly washed, dressed and headed out the door.

***

Emily gently woke her grandfather as the plane taxied to its gate. He had been out cold for most of the flight. It was a relief after the embarrassment at the airport when some stupid lighter he was carrying had set off the metal detector, which resulted in an overwhelming security response. She had wanted to disappear into thin air – or desert him - but she did neither. On the plane, however, he had been so still for so long that she had actually leaned in to check he was still breathing. Her grandfather was tough, everyone knew that, but he was also old, and he hadn't been on an airplane since coming home from Vietnam. Did they even have pressurized aircraft back then? They certainly didn't know what deep vein thrombosis was. She sighed with relief when he stirred from his slumber.

They made their way through customs control to baggage claim. Emily had to admit she was a little disappointed. She wasn't sure what she had expected from the airport, but it was a neon-lit, sterile, concrete structure, probably much like all airports. She could have been in O'Hare rather than Ho Chi Minh City.

The arrivals hall gave hints of what was to come. The bilingual signs and a majority proportion of Vietnamese, rather than Caucasian faces, made it clear they were far from home. The unfamiliar language filled her ears; it was incomprehensible but felt warm and friendly – and everyone seemed to be smiling. Could the Vietnamese be the friendliest people in the world?

Once they had collected their baggage, they trundled toward the exit, and Emily got her first proper look at the people of Vietnam. Some were waiting impatiently for loved ones, some were embracing, some tearful – and some were sullen looking drivers holding up signs This was the area of transition between the familiarity of an airport and the brave new world beyond the doors.

Then they were out into the hot and humid night air where Emily felt a film of sweat cover her skin. Out here, the carefully orchestrated queues of the arrivals hall broke down into a sea of shouting and gesturing. She looked at her grandfather. He looked faint. Was the climate getting to him? Was he having some sort of flashback to the war? A stroke? "Oh, please, don't let him die before we've even made it to the city," she whispered to the gods. She immediately regretted the callous thought and grabbed Tom's hand to reassure him. It was a physical reminder that he was not alone and had her there to help.

Emily guided her dazed and anxious grandfather to a line of taxis and was amazed when he said something in Vietnamese to a trader on the way. They didn't have to wait long to find a driver, and she settled back to absorb what she could in spite of the darkness. At the hotel, they checked in and made their way to their room where they quickly unpacked some essentials and went to bed.

The next morning Emily awoke to the sound of a shower. It took her a few moments to work out where she was. By the time she got her bearings, her grandfather had appeared encased in a towel, just as Jessica had predicted. He gave her a big grin and wished her a jaunty good morning. She nodded back and painted on a smile, silently hoping that this would not become part of their daily routine. Before he could say anything more, she grabbed some clothes and headed for the bathroom.

They made it to the breakfast area with minutes to spare before it closed. "I'll have some coffee, white toast and scrambled eggs," Tom said politely to the Vietnamese waiter.

Emily was underwhelmed. You could have that in any diner in America. She was on a journey; it was time to travel with her taste buds as well as her legs. "What would *you* have for breakfast?" Emily asked the waiter.

"Pho," he replied neutrally.

"I'll have that then, and some coffee," she said, feeling a little smug.

Tom stopped the waiter to add, "And please bring some sugar, not sweetener, for the coffee."

They talked about the flight until the waiter brought Tom his order and placed a steaming bowl of meat and noodles in front of Emily. She realized that coffee was probably not the best drink to compliment this, but she was ready for a new experience.

"Are you sure you want the local stuff?" Tom asked, looking skeptically at her bowl. "Ninety-two million Vietnamese can't be wrong," Emily said defiantly and scooped up some noodles. The broth was hot and spicy, but the noodles were tender and tasty. After finishing the first mouthful, she went for another, this time taking some meat. She hoped it was chicken or pork but suddenly wondered if it could be dog … or was that a Korean thing? Was she racist even thinking this? As her mind considered culinary racism, her mouth signaled a problem. Not only was the broth hot in temperature, but the spices were potent too. Her mouth was on fire. She coughed and spluttered. "Water," she croaked.

"No, you need to swallow this," her grandfather said, handing her two open sachets. Her need beyond any regard for dignity, she snatched them from his hand and dumped them in her mouth.

"Swirl it around your mouth; it will absorb the spice." She obeyed his calm instructions. "Now rinse it down with some of that coffee."

Emily moved her tongue around her mouth; the searing heat was gone. It was a miracle. Perhaps her grandfather wouldn't be the liability she had feared.

"What did you just give me?" Emily asked, her eyes full of tears from the spicy pho.

"Sugar," Tom said matter-of-factly.

"No way!" Emily protested.

"Yeah, the sugar absorbs the spice like a sponge, and then you rinse it away with a drink. Not everything I learned in-country was combat oriented. Still, you were always safe with C-rations," Tom said, biting into his toast as a form of emphatic punctuation.

Emily signaled the waiter, who approached to ask, "Did you like the pho?" She couldn't tell if he had witnessed her disastrous pho introduction or if his air of innocence was genuine.

"It was great, but I'm not used to that for breakfast," she replied and, looking at her grandfather's plate said, "I'll have what he's having."

After breakfast, they took a taxi to Tao Dan Park. Tom had been most insistent on going and, centrally located as it was, it seemed like a good place to start. It turned out to be a spacious public park with bench-lined paths, a Buddhist temple, and large, shady trees, a welcome oasis of calm and a refuge from the bustling streets. It was busy this morning, full of all ages playing sports, jogging and doing tai chi. It was also a bird watcher's paradise; some even 'walked' their feathered pets in their cages. Children squealed and ran around, relishing the freedom of the open space, while others sat on benches, chatting and people-watching.

Emily noticed the slight frown and the faraway look in her grandfather's eyes. He seemed to be remembering something, and the look on his face implied it wasn't good.

"Has it changed much?" Emily enquired.

"The park, no, the people … it's good to see that humans can survive almost anything."

***

While Tom and the squad had been loading the M113 APCs, a G.I. in an immaculate new uniform, laden down with full kit and pack, stood nearby watching. They noticed him but were too busy to bother with someone who was nothing to do with their imminent mission.

"What's the deal, soldier?" Skoberne asked, motioning the G.I. to come closer. He was anxious to get going and didn't want any pointless distractions.

"Sir, Private Gregory Chapman reporting for duty, sir."

"You're kidding, a replacement, just as we're heading out on an operation?"

"Sir, it would seem that way, sir."

"Alright, get in the back of that APC." Before Skoberne could say anything else, the fresh-faced soldier turned for the armored vehicle. "And for god's sake, take that pack off and stow it; you're going into combat, not on a camping trip," Skoberne bellowed after him.

Tom and the rest of the squad followed Chapman into the M113 and closed the hatch after them. The APC lurched forward, and they held on grimly for the rough hour-long drive to Saigon.

"Hey, cherry!" Mo shouted over the roar of the engine to Chapman, who was fussing with his pack and rifle.

"Uh, yes?"

"We are about to go on possibly our toughest operation to date."

"Ah, okay."

"So just do what we tell you to do as soon as we tell you to do it, or you'll get either yourself or, more importantly, one of us killed," Eddie instructed.

Chapman blushed furiously and nothing else was said. The atmosphere was grim and determined as the men triple-checked their equipment in their claustrophobic steel tomb. A chance for payback was coming. The enemy had revealed itself in broad daylight and in full force. It was time to neutralize the feelings of fear and impotence that had been gnawing away at each and every one of them.

The APCs clattered and groaned as they pulled to a stop at the edge of Tao Dan Park. Alabama opened the hatch and the men disgorged from the belly of the beast. Until just hours ago, the park would have been busy with people enjoying its beautiful, leafy-green spaces, but now it was deserted. The sounds of war had come to the city of Saigon, and the streets were eerily quiet as the residents took refuge in their homes. The soldiers fanned out as they made their way across the park. VC had been sighted in the area and a military police jeep had come under fire from a nearby building. Tom stuck close to Eddie to help him with the cumbersome M60 and its ammo.

"I can't get used to all the plastic on this rifle," Chapman said.

"You can tell it's Mattel," Ortiz replied sarcastically, referencing a toy advert that many G.I.s had muttered when handling the M16 for the first time.

"Shut up, Chapman," Tom snapped. The men needed to focus 100 percent on what they were doing. So far, the cherry had only shown himself to be a liability.

Just then, shots rang out. Some enemy soldiers had positioned themselves on the opposite side of the park and started firing at the Americans. Captain de Bruin gave the order to return fire, and the APCs got to work, firing their 50 cal heavy machine guns, the boom of the ammunition echoing around the park like a raging predator on the hunt. The shells blasting from the APCs produced shockwaves powerful enough to do damage without even hitting their targets.

Tom moved forward and spotted a man kneeling by a tree; he was wearing a white shirt, tan trousers and flip-flops. He looked like any other young man in Saigon, except he was shouldering an AK47, and he was aiming it at Lieutenant Skoberne.

Tom aimed and fired off three rounds. One hit just above the man's head and burrowed into the tree, but the other two struck him on the side of the head and neck. He went down like a deflating hot air balloon, his weapon hitting the ground beside his collapsing corpse.

The thud of a nearby explosion caused Ramirez to fire his m79 and take out a man who was using an upturned wheelbarrow for cover. The shockwave from the grenade reverberated around them, its noise bouncing off the walls of the surrounding buildings.

"Get that pig firing, private," Skoberne yelled at Eddie, who was checking that the belt of ammunition was straight so he could lay down suppressing fire. He blasted away at two men on either side of a tree, bullets from his M60 ripping bark and wood splinters from their cover. Alabama, Mo and Chapman shot at them, and they fell limp under the hail of bullets.

"I got one!" Chapman exclaimed excitedly.

"Shut up FNG; those were mine and Alabama's kills," Mo barked at him.

While Mo was the more experienced soldier, his Stevens Model 77E shotgun was less likely to have killed the enemy than Chapman's longer range weapon, but the new recruit didn't have the confidence to challenge him. Chapman dropped his eyes and said nothing more.

The soldiers carried out a flanking maneuver. The APCs and the two machine gunners in the platoon laid down suppressing fire as the rest of the troops attacked from the sides. The fierce firefight filled the empty streets with the sounds of battle. The VC had no idea how to neutralize the assault, and they were quickly cut down by the soldiers' gunfire.

"I'm hit!" called out Corporal Ventura. The wound initially looked serious; the bullet had grazed the side of his neck, tearing off his earlobe. There was a lot of blood, but he would be fine and back in rotation within the week, with a Purple Heart for his troubles. This contact would be recorded as eight enemy dead, zero Americans killed or wounded. It had been a good contact.

The men moved on, away from the safety of the APC fire arcs and across the deserted main road, into the side streets and more buildings. A shot rang out and a soldier fell to the ground, his shoulder pierced by a 7.62 round fired by a Dragunov sniper rifle. This was the start of the second contact.

"Sniper!" Ortiz called out. He was radioing an update of the situation into HQ while the platoon fanned out to different streets and houses. Another shot rang out, kicking up dirt as the medic tried to get to the wounded man.

"Looks like the shots are coming from this building," Tom said, pointing to the apartment block where they were crouched.

"Let's go in," Alabama said, ready to go.

"Check your corners; make sure each apartment is properly cleared before we move on - and keep moving so Charlie doesn't have time to plant any booby traps," Skoberne said as the soldiers cautiously filed in.

Eddie, with his long and heavy M60, was forced to cover the hallway as his weapon wasn't designed for this sort of close-quarters' operation. He lay on the floor at the very end of the corridor and watched for any movement as the rest of the team advanced.

"Fourth floor, five windows in. I think that's where the sniper is located. Over," a voice crackled from Ortiz's radio.

The medic back in the park had spotted movement near an open window. All the civilians would have been hugging the floor, and the elevation was perfect for overlooking the park. Skoberne radioed an affirmative back and ordered the men to move upward. Another shot rang out. The sniper was hunting for targets. There was a sporadic return of fire as the Americans yelled out the sniper's likely location. Tom and the squad carefully crept up the stairwell, each man covering a potential angle of fire. As they got closer to the fourth floor, they became quieter until only their breathing could be heard. Eddie brought up the rear, pointing his beast of a machine gun down the stairway in case somebody came at them from below. Chapman was awed at how smoothly the squad worked together. He clearly had a lot of catching up to do. After a few minutes, they arrived on the fourth floor.

"Five windows in. I reckon that's the second apartment on the left," Ortiz whispered.

Skoberne nodded in agreement and pulled out his sidearm. At such close quarters, Mo with the shotgun and Skoberne with his pistol would be the most effective. The soldiers grouped around the door of the apartment. Edde set up his machine gun to cover the stairwell. Ortiz knelt and covered the other side of the hall. The rest of the squad stared at the apartment door as if it was a coiled snake ready to strike.

Mo knocked the lock out of the door with a point-blank blast from the shotgun. Skoberne kicked the door, and the two of them moved in, with the rest of the squad covering the short hallway. An AK47 snapped around the corner and blind- fired down the hall. The soldiers dodged for cover or swung around door frames to escape the high-velocity hail of bullets.

Mo fired at the rifle and the barely visible hand gripping it. The pellets from the shotgun peppered the robust weapon and tore it from the man's hand. There was a cry of pain, and the bloodied hand disappeared as the rifle clattered to the floor.

"Move up on them," Skoberne ordered.

"Man down!" Ortiz called out.

The men all looked back and saw that Chapman, who had been standing in the line of fire, had taken two in the chest and one in the stomach. He was lying awkwardly, his head and shoulders propped up on the wall opposite the doorway and the rest of his body crumpled on the floor. Blood was rapidly darkening his green uniform. Chapman stared at them in wide-eyed disbelief. He coughed up some blood and, after a couple of shallow breaths, lay still, the light fading from his eyes.

There was nothing the men could do for him, but now the fight with the sniper's nest of VC had become personal. Nobody knew Chapman and, truth be told, he was an annoying cherry, but he was their cherry, and a commie had just killed an American. That was not going to go unpunished. Eddie looked after Chapman's body while the others moved in for the kill.

The men moved forward in a grimly determined manner. They were no longer soldiers but judge, jury and executioners on a hunt for the guilty, and everyone in this apartment was guilty. Their ugly mood was shattered by a storm of lead that bellowed at them from outside. One of the APCs had moved up and was now blasting the window and the wall around it with its 50 caliber ammunition. The shells pulverized the concrete and, with a deafening roar, exploded into the apartment. Skoberne didn't have to order anyone to get down; they all embraced the floor as if it was a lover.

Skoberne pointed to Ortiz and waved his open hand over his throat signaling for the APC to stop firing in case they were all killed in a friendly-fire incident. Ortiz nodded and began to crawl away from the 50 caliber hurricane so he could be heard over the deafening roar of the heavy machine gun fire. After a few seconds of frantic radio contact, the APC stopped blasting at the side of the apartment block.

Tom opened his mouth trying to get his ears to pop; the 50 caliber rounds had been so loud he wanted to check he still had eardrums. Apart from the whistling in his ears, the silence was broken only by the sound of loose plaster and shards of glass hitting the floor. It was as if the gunfire had swept away sound itself. Dust hung in the air and covered the men where they lay. It clung to everything, and Tom began to cough when he inhaled some that caught in his throat.

The soldiers got up again and began to feed through the apartment. The Viet Cong who had blind-fired around the corner turned out to be a woman who had been cut almost in half by the hail of bullets With such massive wounds, she was probably dead before she hit the floor. Tom spotted movement by a chair as a man reached for his rifle. Without hesitation, Tom fired four rounds and killed him.

Alabama signaled he'd found a third body. This guy was missing half his head as he'd taken a direct hit from the 50 cal. In the space of two minutes, an apartment in downtown Saigon had been turned into a butcher's yard. The front room was scarred and blasted; its shattered windows stared with fractured eyes, a silent witness to the horrors of war. Three enemy dead to one American. The kill count was acceptable in military terms.

The men returned to Chapman, his dead eyes now staring lifelessly back at them. Tom squatted down and closed them; now he looked peaceful. While the others provided cover in case of another attack, Tom and Alabama carried Chapman downstairs. They were unconcerned with the occupants of the building; their only focus was the enemy.

Chapman's dead body was loaded into the back of the same APC he had arrived in alive less than an hour ago, his corpse now resting next to the pack that he would never open.

***

Tom gazed at the building where all of this had happened, the blasted wall and shattered windows long since repaired. Part of the front was now obscured by a billboard showing a smiling woman and an image of toothpaste. She seemed to be smiling at him.

"Excuse me," the heavily accented English forced Tom from his reflections. He looked over and saw a middle-aged Vietnamese man approaching with a smile. Did everyone here smile all the time Tom wondered.

"Yes?" Tom responded. Emily moved closer to Tom, not sure what was happening.

"We get many visitors here in Ho Chi Minh City but not so many in this park, and I have never seen any of them stare so intently at my mother's apartment building. Forgive my boldness, but you're Americans, aren't you?"

Tom nodded while his brain churned over the information. Was the man standing in front of him a physical link to his past? "Does your mother live in that building?"

"Oh, yes, in fact, she's right over there," the man said, pointing to a petite, gray-haired woman, sitting on a nearby bench and enjoying the sunshine as she watched the children playing.

"Do you think I could talk to your mother?" Tom asked, so intent on the pursuit of his memories that he seemed to be acting without thinking.

"Grandpa, no!" exclaimed Emily.

"Sweetheart, it's okay," Tom replied reassuringly.

"She cannot speak English, but I can translate," the man said with an approving nod.

Then, remembering his manners, Tom reached out to shake hands as he introduced himself and his granddaughter. "I'm Tom and this is Emily," he said as Long responded in kind, and the three of them walked over to his mother. More introductions, more smiles. Tom needed to tread carefully. He didn't want to lie but he couldn't tell the whole truth either, so he commented only that he had seen the building when it seemed damaged beyond repair.

Long's mother had vivid memories of that time, and Long translated her version of the day the Americans attacked her home. She and her husband had just married, but he had had to leave almost immediately because he was an officer in the ARVN. She had stayed behind in their third-floor apartment, crying and praying for him every day. Then the Americans arrived in their tanks and began firing on the building. The noise was deafening and she felt the whole building shake, but she didn't see much as she lay under the bed, the safest place she could think of. Gunfire shattered the bedroom window. As it came closer, she stopped praying for her husband and started praying for herself. Later, she felt ashamed that she had been so worried about her own life when her husband was in far more danger every day. When it was all over, she discovered that neighbors had been killed and other apartments had been damaged or destroyed. Frightened and alone, she fled to relatives in another part of the city where she stayed throughout the war.

As she recounted the story, Tom felt a swell of shame but said nothing about his direct involvement in the events that had devastated her home. He and his squad had been so intent on hunting down Charlie that they hadn't spared a moment's thought for the civilian lives around them. Long's mother spoke matter-of-factly and gave no hint that she held any hatred for the Americans when her building was briefly, but brutally turned into a war zone. What happened on that day was bad enough, but things got worse after the fall of Saigon in 1975.

When his mother fell silent, Long took up the story. His mother had been pregnant with him in 1975. After the initial waves of attacks, Long's father realized that South Vietnam was going to collapse. The Americans were leaving, and his father tried desperately to get his family out of the country. He managed to get airline tickets to Ottowa, Canada, but the NVA attacked the runway and cut off that means of escape. They had queued for an airlift by American forces but were too far back in the line and failed to get on board. He tried everything he could think of, but once the last choppers had flown off into the distance, he resigned himself to the inevitability of capture.

The tyrannical communist regime, which had been brutal throughout the war, was barbaric in victory and inflicted appalling suffering on the population of the south. Long's father, along with some 300,000 others, was incarcerated in what amounted to a concentration camp for 're-education'. The privations broke him during five years of hardship. His crime? He had fought on the losing side of the war. To make matters worse, Vietnam had been invaded by China and had seen its economy collapse. When Long's father returned to his family, he found they were suffering almost as badly as those in the camps.

Emily could see the tears welling up in her grandfather's eyes. He had something to do with all of this, but she wasn't sure what – and her grandfather was giving nothing away. Long and his mother were interested to know that Tom had seen the building in its damaged state but did not press him on the circumstances. Given all that had happened afterward, it was, for them, just another incident in a bigger family tragedy. Maybe they were willing to let the past remain in the past, but Emily was fixed on the mother's account. She had been on the receiving end of American gunfire that had no regard for the innocent occupants of a building under their bombardment. Was her grandfather a killer? She didn't know what to think.

Emily was deep in thought when Long brought their story up-to-date. His was the first generation to grow up in a unified and communist Vietnam. The past of Long's father was the family's shame and, as such, despite being an exemplary student, Long had struggled to get a good job. He worked for the city's power grid in a role that he was overqualified to do and underpaid to carry out. Still, it was a regular income, which was important once he had a family. His mother had been a widow for ten years, and

Long visited her regularly, keenly aware of his filial responsibilities, especially as he had no brothers or sisters.

Despite his traumatic family history, Long was hopeful for the future. Yes, Vietnam was still a dictatorial regime, but as memories of the war faded, the need to punish the children of those labeled 'war criminals' also faded; the younger generation was anxious to leave the war in the past. The country was opening up, progress was being made and the economy had picked up. Long was optimistic.

Emily had stepped back from the conversation, both physically and emotionally. Heartbreaking as the stories were, she wanted to keep her distance, to remove herself from a dark reality she knew involved her grandfather. As the conversation came to a close and farewells were being said, Long felt compelled to observe, "Many Americans come here to make a connection with their past and to pay their respects to the dead. I think you are doing the same."

"Yes, I suppose I am."

Long handed him a card. "This is my number; I would be happy to help you with anything you need – maybe act as a guide while you're in our city."

"Thank you," Tom said, taking the card and shaking his hand. "It's funny, even though I've been in your country for only a day, I've spent longer talking with you than I did with any Vietnamese when I was here for over a year."

***

After they left the park, Tom was preoccupied with the morning's events, happy to follow Emily around a nearby market. To him, everything looked like garish junk, but Emily fell in love with a pair of sunglasses, knock-off Ray-Bans, and a purse that was, apparently, 'too cute'. She was enthusiastic about her purchases, overly so thought Tom, but she had little to say to him. She was polite but cool. Something was up.

As the morning's activities began to take their toll on Tom's energy and Emily's stomach, they agreed to find somewhere to eat and opted for the noodle bar with the most garishly illustrated photos. The place was busy and full of locals, always a good sign. Some of the diners giving them curious stares as they picked their way through the tightly-packed tables to a vacant spot in the corner. Then, after much gesticulating, some sign language and snatched words of Vietnamese from Google Translate on Emily's phone, they managed to get bowls of pork, vegetables and rice noodles that were spicy without burning the insides of their mouths. Tom decided it was time to tackle his granddaughter's distant attitude. "Okay, sweetheart, what's with the long face?"

Emily was so surprised by the question she spluttered and nearly spat out her mouthful. She was glad she had the time it took to recover to think of a decent response, but she came out with a lame, "Nothing," said unconvincingly. Was that really the best she could come up with? She was disappointed in her own lack of imagination.

"C'mon, you can talk to me."

"I didn't come here to help you bury the past!" Emily blurted out.

It was Tom's turn to be surprised. He'd been so involved in his plans he hadn't stopped to consider that Emily had her own reasons for the trip. He remembered that she had been less than enthusiastic about traveling with him and that he had agreed they could split up, but he'd thought they'd do the tourist things together, then, maybe, she would agree to visit places from his past. "I'm sorry. I didn't think. It's just that since your grandmother died, my time here has come back to haunt me. Things I haven't really thought about for decades are with me all the time now. I feel like I have to do something about them before they stifle me, but I didn't mean to drag you into all of this. And, of course, I had no idea that we would meet people in the park who …" he trailed off.

Emily sighed, put down her chopsticks and leaned forward. "Grandpa, what I heard today shocked me." She paused. He had asked, so she decided to tell him what was on her mind. "No, it was more than that. It shocked *and* disgusted me."

Tom had guessed it was going to be something like this. The stories had been hard to hear, but instead of commenting, he stayed silent and let her continue.

"The Americans had a gun battle in the midst of people's homes! … the destruction, the slaughter … it's just, it's …" Emily struggled to find the words. Then, "I know you were there; I know you were involved and it makes me feel sick!" The floodgates opened, and Emily's pent-up emotions were spilling out. Tom watched her and listened in silence. "It's just that you're my grandfather, and I can't believe you were part of this! Then all the other stuff about the

Americans abandoning Long and his family to their fate at the hands of the communists. How could you? How could anyone do that?"

Tom's shoulders slumped and his head dropped. He had heard all of this before, but not for a long time and never from his grandchild. His legacy was one of dishonor, shame and regret; her stinging condemnation cut holes in his heart. Could she ever forgive him? More importantly, *should* she forgive him? Was forgiveness even possible after all the things he had done? He wished Elaine was here; she was always much better with words than he was. Instead of her consoling presence, he faced this angry young woman alone.

"Didn't you learn anything about the war in school?" Tom asked as if a history lesson could explain everything.

"Yeah, a bit, but it wasn't, like, a topic that resonated."

"We thought we were saving not just Vietnam, but that entire region from communism. It was called the 'domino theory' – that if one country fell, others would follow. This was happening at the time of the so-called Cold War with the Soviet Union, and we saw communism as a worldwide threat that had to be stopped before it went any further. Our downfall was that we understood nothing about the region, nothing about the people, their culture or their history, and we got it badly wrong. The simple truth is that the Vietnamese were caught between two ruthless rivalries, neither one of which they wanted to win. While those in the south feared the communist regime, it promised them land, and for a population of peasants that meant survival. But if they feared the communists, they hated their own corrupt regime which was propped up by the Americans simply because it was not communist. It had no political authority and never had the support of the people, so it was a war we were never going to win. Not that we knew that at the time. I don't know at what point our leaders understood this, but they let it go on for decades because no one wanted to be the first to lose an American war. Those of us who fought were as cruelly deceived and as cruelly sacrificed as the people here," Tom concluded angrily.

"Of course I knew you were in the war, but as a kid, I didn't understand what it meant. Now I'm here and confronted with the reality, I can't begin to put you into that context. It's too much, too confusing; you expect too much of me!" Emily exploded. People were turning to look at them. Tom reached out to take her hand, but she snatched it away, glowering at him.

"Keep it calm, Em. You know, there's one expression I learned when I was in-country: he who raises his voice loses the argument. It stuck with me because it was such an un-American way of looking at things."

Emily looked around at the Vietnamese diners who, seeing that the show was over, went back to their food and conversations.

Tom took a deep breath and said, "Let's start from the beginning. Let me tell you exactly what happened so you can condemn me with facts." So Tom told her everything, just as he had remembered it in the park, and concluded by saying, "There it is, just as it happened. I'm making no excuses except to say that it was war."

"I know you aren't a naturally violent or aggressive person. Couldn't you just get out of it ... somehow?"

"Listen, right now you're a little older than I was back then. How would you feel, right now, if you were told you had to join the army or go to jail?"

"But that's not going to happen," Emily said defensively.

"But it happened to me when I was about your age." Tom allowed that to sink in before continuing, "Many of the young Americans who came here to fight weren't old enough to buy a beer back home. The average age of a combat soldier in Vietnam was nineteen. There was a strange pop song about that back in the 1980s. Your mother loved it and made me listen to it, but I guess that came out a decade before you were born."

"I have no idea what you're talking about."

"Okay, let me put it another way. I guess you've seen some of the films about Vietnam, right?"

"Yes, a couple. They aren't really my kinda thing."

"One of my issues with them is that they used actors in their twenties and thirties, so it looks like mature men were fighting this war. But a fair few of our majors, that's a step up from captain, were still in their twenties. We were a bunch of ignorant kids running around the jungle, being told what to do by an even more ignorant government halfway across the world. We were scared all the time. We were scared of going to war, of getting killed, of letting the squad down, of coming back a freak with no legs - but we were even more scared of our leaders who seemed, to put it bluntly, clueless."

"You may have been ignorant kids, but you caused death and destruction," Emily argued, conceding nothing.

"War *is* death and destruction; that's what the word means. Do you think we were giving out hugs in World War II or the Civil War?"

"But they were different."

"How? Tell me. Just because those wars were long ago doesn't mean there was less in the way of carnage. Of course, slavery was immoral and the Nazis were evil, but it wasn't just bad people who died in those wars. It was General Sherman, a Union general, supposedly one of the 'good guys', who destroyed Georgia with his march to the sea. I'm pretty sure the residents of Atlanta didn't think it was justified. Still don't. You name me a war, any war, and there will be documented numbers of dead from both sides, and a list of shattered towns and cities, and a host of grievances still being played out. Whatever battlefield achievements there are for the military, it's the civilians who always lose."

"But none of those wars included my grandfather!" Emily exclaimed in a loud whisper, trying not to attract any more attention.

Tom paused. He was trying to explain the inexplicable, and it was falling on ears that could not hear. His darling Emily

… she had grown into such a fine young woman, but she was still new to the world. "I'm sorry, but you're going to find out worse about me and the men I served with … *if* you decide to come with me on this journey," he said quietly as the image of the woman flashed before him once again. Would he have the strength to tell her about that?

"I guess women didn't have to make these choices," Emily replied feebly.

"There were American nurses in Vietnam, brave women who had to tend to the wounded under artillery and mortar fire. We loved to catch glimpses of them. Vietnamese girls are pretty, but we got tired of seeing almond-shaped eyes and dark hair. Blonde-haired, blue-eyes nurses … well, that was a glimpse of home, that would keep us happy for days, longer if we got to talk to them."

"Jesus, Grandpa, sexist *and* racist all in one sentence!"

"Oh, excuse me. Apparently young male soldiers, who put their lives at risk on a daily basis, should also act like monks."

"You know what I mean," Emily said, crossing her arms defiantly.

"Well, if I do, then you know what I mean. Soldiers will be soldiers and men will be men; your grandmother and I had a fully functioning marital relationship; we had two kids the old-fashioned way," Tom said with the trace of a smile.

"Oh, God, no! I don't want my head full of images of my grandparents having sex!"

"Well, better that than the image of your grandfather as a war criminal!"

They glared at each other and fell silent for the rest of the meal.

***

Jessica was wandering around Krogers, looking for inspiration. When she found herself in cereals, she paused to consider not just the vast array, but the ridiculousness of some on offer. Were neon colors suitable for breakfast foods? Apparently, Lucky Charms now came with rainbow marshmallows. How did anyone get to the point of thinking that marshmallows were a suitable food choice to start the day?

As she meandered around the isles, Jessica flicked through the apps on her phone. She was worried about her friend. She followed Emily on her Instagram account where she had posted photos of herself in some park in Ho Chi Minh City and, later, hilariously trying out different sunglasses and asking her followers which ones best suited her, all cool filters and matching attitude. If you knew Em only via Instagram, you'd assume she was having the time of her life, but what was interesting to Jess was that there was never any mention of her grandfather. Unless you knew she had gone with him, it was like he didn't exist. Emily had done a very good job of expunging him from her travel narrative, which, according to Instagram, was the story of one young woman traveling on her own and having an amazing time in Vietnam.

But Jessica was also using WhatsApp to pick up Emily's messages. According to these, Em's grandfather had totally hijacked the trip to make a return journey to his brutal past, and she was in the depths of despair. From waking up and seeing him emerge half-naked from the shower (Jess smiled to herself in a told-you-so way) to listening to him relive some gun battle in an apartment building, the messages signaled ever more desperation. It sounded worse than root canal surgery, especially as this was supposed to be the trip of a lifetime, something her friend had been saving up for over months. Jessica was worried; she couldn't shake the anxiety that gripped her every time a new message appeared on her phone. Emily was sinking into depression and didn't know how to escape.

Lost in her phone, Jessica had stopped in the midst of cereals where she was now considering the multitude of options, when she looked up and spied Sarah, Emily's mother, inspecting a box of Cheerios Oat Crisps. What did this say about the woman? That variety of Cheerios was high in fiber and low in saturated fats, but if she was worried about her carb intake, she should be going for the reduced sugar option. Jessica caught herself mid-thought; perhaps her cereal obsession was getting a little out of hand. "Hello, Mrs. Hawkins," Jessica said, waving and walking toward Em's mother.

Sarah turned her attention away from the label she was reading and looked up. "Oh, hello, Jessica, how are you?"

"Fine, thank you. I was sorry to hear you lost your mother."

"Thank you. I guess you know all about that from Emily."

"Yes, it was hard for her to lose her grandmother; it must have been hard for you, too," Jessica offered.

"Yes, but it wasn't unexpected, not that this ever makes things easier. But tell me, what are you up to these days? Emily told me you were looking at nursing positions in the city."

"I've had an offer I'm considering but, honestly, I'm not sure. I guess I'd always assumed Em and I would find jobs together. Now that she's gone, I'm kind of … unsettled, not sure what I want to do." Then, "You must be missing her."

"Yes, of course, but it's not as bad as it might be. If it were either Emily or my father out there on their own, I would be worried sick. Instead, I know they're looking after each other, so that's reassuring. I hear from Emily regularly, and she seems to be having a great time."

That would be the parentally linked Facebook account thought Jessica. Did parents not realize they were being fed a selective and highly polished version of events and that nothing that wholesome could possibly be real? Jessica caught herself breaking into a knowing smile and wiped it from her face. She remembered getting Emily to take a photo of her in church and then posting it on her Facebook page so that her parents would think she was going again. They bought it, which was weird because she hadn't gone to church since she was twelve.

Jessica could play along or she could share her concerns with Mrs. Hawkins. Interfering in the dynamics of another family was a minefield, but her worries outweighed any considerations she had for Em's confidences. "Mrs. Hawkins ..."

"Oh, Jessica, you girls are all grown up now, so I think it's time you called me Sarah."

"Um … okay, Sarah. Excuse me for saying so, but I'm not so sure your daughter *is* having a great time."

Sarah cocked her head quizzically. This was news to her, but Jessica seemed sincere and, realistically, she probably knew more about what was going on. "What do you mean?"

"Well, this vacation was supposed to be the trip of a lifetime for Em. We both know how hard she worked to save up for it, but her plans never included her grandpa, y'know?"

"Emily loves him."

"Of course she does, but it's one thing to love someone and another thing to travel together."

" … mmm … I guess you have a point. I just thought this trip might be the answer for both of them. He's been lost since my mother died – and well - with the two of them traveling together, I didn't have to worry about either of them being on their own."

"I can see why you thought this was a good idea," Jess said cautiously, "but I think the problem is that they have very different reasons for traveling. He's trying to come to terms with the loss of his wife while traveling in a place that must have traumatized him when he was there, whereas Em is trying to figure out what she wants to do with the rest of her life."

"When you put it that way, it really doesn't make much sense, does it … the two of them traveling together? I guess I didn't stop to consider how her grandfather's presence would impact her plans." Sarah clutched the cereal box as if it was a security blanket. "What has she said to you?"

Jessica hesitated, not sure how much to reveal. "It's not so much what she says as the feeling I get that her grandfather has pretty much taken over the trip. He seems to be setting the agenda, and she doesn't feel she can say anything. Plus she can't strike off on her own or explore the things that interest her because she feels responsible for him."

Sarah nodded her acknowledgment. Jessica was surprisingly astute for one so young. Feeling embarrassed at her own shortcomings in the matter, Sarah shifted the conversation and said, "You must be missing Emily, too."

Jessica laughed and waved her phone. "Yes, but nowadays, it's possible to be in touch all the time."

Sarah smiled as she put the box of Cheerios Oat Crisps in her trolley. "Well, I must be off, but it was nice to see you, Jessica. Let's keep in touch while Emily is away."

"I'd like that, Mrs. Hawkins – Sarah. "Oh and if you're worried about your sugar intake, I recommend these," Jessica said, reaching over to take the low sugar Cheerios from the shelf.

***

Lieutenant Skoberne had just finished a briefing with Captain de Bruin, and his face was grim with the news. His squad had been back at camp resting and re-equipping, memories of the firefight in Saigon still fresh in their minds ... as was the memory of Chapman's lifeless body. They were all too aware of the possibility that they could share his fate; it was just a shame nobody could remember his name.

Now they were busy preparing for what came next, but they hadn't missed the look on their lieutenant's face. "What is it, sir?" asked Alabama.

"Huế, we've recaptured the city."

"That's good news, isn't it, sir?"

"Yes, it is, but it's what they've found: mass graves, hundreds of bodies. Men, women, children, probably seen as collaborators."

"Jesus Christ! Even children?" Tom exploded.

"Wrong god, right reaction," Eddie retorted.

"Ain't the gooks Buddhists?" Mo asked, addressing no one in particular.

"Not relevant, private," snapped Skoberne who took his helmet off and wiped his brow, partly to remove the sweat, but mainly to soothe his weariness. "Just when you think this place can't get any more savage ..." he muttered under his breath as he stalked off. His last comment was drowned out by the noise coming from a trio of choppers approaching overhead. He pulled out a cigarette and lit it, a comforting act of normality on a very abnormal day.

As Skoberne made his way through the sticky brown mud, heading toward the officers' mess, he saw two soldiers approaching. It took him a moment to recognize the men because, while he knew the faces, one in particular very well, he was not expecting to see either of them again.

"Sergeant Zielinski," Skoberne said, saluting.

"Sir," the sergeant said, replying with his own crisp salute and the merest hint of a wince of pain.

Skoberne noted his long sleeves were all the way down and buttoned at the cuffs. This was, presumably, a ruse to cover the burns on his arm, but the lieutenant noticed those on his right hand. Was he able to perform his duties? The truth was immaterial. Skoberne knew that short of having his head taken off by the VC, Zielinski would keep coming back for more. But there was no denying that the lieutenant was glad to see the bravest and most experienced soldier in the whole company. Turning to the other soldier, Skoberne smiled and saluted, saying, "Corporal Ventura."

"Sir," Ventura replied, returning the salute. The corporal was minus an earlobe but was otherwise absolutely fine. It was ironic that the purple heart he received for being wounded in action weighed more than the little piece of flesh he had lost. Aware that Zielinski had suffered far worse injuries but had received no medal, Ventura had hidden his. He didn't believe he deserved it, believed that wearing it devalued it to a worthless piece of tin. Saying that, Ventura had heard the sergeant had won the purple heart twice - and a bronze star, too.

"I tell you, as soon as I leave the platoon, the whole country goes to hell. I understand I missed some real action in Saigon," Zielinski said with his usual air of indestructible confidence.

"I'm not going to lie; it was good to have the enemy in front of us, no jungle to hide in. We cut through them like a scythe at harvest time," Skoberne replied with a satisfied little smile.

"Too bad that's not the way the civilian press back home is reporting it, sir. Even though we've crushed the commies, everyone is wailing about how the war is now unwinnable."

Skoberne raised an eyebrow. Unwinnable? How was that possible after such a major victory? Besides, didn't America always win its wars? "Are you ready to go back on rotation?" Skoberne asked, knowing the answer.

"Of course, sir. I'd like to see how the squad is doing if that's okay," Zielinski said, obviously itching to return to normal.

"Yes, get on over to them now; they've missed you, we all have," Skoberne said, turning to Corporal Ventura to give him orders to report to his commanding officer. Ventura headed off, his enthusiastic gait slowed by the mud. Skoberne continued his trudge back to the officers' mess while Zielinski arrived at his squad's large tented area.

Eddie's record player was blaring out 'Fire' by Jimi Hendrix in an attempt to drown out Mo's sermonizing about black power. It wasn't that Eddie didn't agree with Mo, it was just that Mo had a way of ranting rather than being persuasive. As Mo tried to drown out the sound of Hendrix, Eddie retaliated by increasing the volume, a gleeful smile on his face. All this was going on when Zielinski came through the tent flaps.

"What the hell is that goddamned racket?" Zielinski barked in his commanding voice.

The men jumped in shock. Eddie moved hastily to switch off his music. Mo was petrified, frozen in fear at the thought of the reprimand he was about to receive from the one white man he both respected and trusted. But the soldiers couldn't contain their smiles. Zielinski's return was good news; everything felt better, more under control, but to acknowledge that would only result in a rebuke and probably some minor punishment.

They all scrambled to their cots and stood to attention. Zielinski strode slowly and deliberately along the row. They were a typical squad, the same kind of men he had been dealing with since Korea. It was hard to say if they were the best, but they were far from the worst. He could have held a grudge against Ortiz. After all, it was his distraction that led to the burns, but the sergeant knew that version of the truth was a dishonest one. Even as a boy he had known that explosives and fire don't mix. He should have been focused on what he was doing.

"I hear you've been busy chasing nurses during my brief time away," Zielinski declared and a got a chuckle from the squad. "I am going to unpack my kit, and when I'm back in seven minutes, I will be conducting a full inspection. I want to see the sun glinting off the steel of your weapons, ladies."

And with that, he turned around and headed off to mentally reconnect with the platoon and put his stupidity behind him. He knew that in war there was no time to second guess the past.

***

Long was eating with the family when his cell phone rang. He didn't recognize the number and was about to let it ring out when he wondered if it might be the Americans. He shushed the family to be quiet. It never worked, so he answered the phone as he got up to leave the table. "Ah-lo?"

"Hi, is this Long?"

"Yes, is that Tom?"

It was. Chau gestured to Long that he shouldn't leave the table in the middle of a family meal. Long waved it away. He had made a connection with the American, which he knew could only be a good thing; Chau would eventually be pleased. Long and Tom chatted for a few minutes before Tom asked if Long had time to be their guide. "Of course, we would pay you," he said, before continuing to explain that they were enjoying the sights in the city, but that he wanted to get out to the countryside. He was particularly interested in a village in the Ap Trai Bí area, but he didn't think he could manage the trip without help.

Long considered: he hadn't anticipated leaving the city, so he would have to take some vacation days and move some shifts around, but it would be worth it. He liked Tom and he welcomed the opportunity to use his English and expand his vocabulary. And the extra income would be useful.

Long sensed that Tom was weighed down by guilt and sorrow. He was not a religious man, but he felt compelled to do what he could to ease Tom's trip to the past. He wasn't sure why the granddaughter had come along. She seemed distant, but that was understandable considering that her grandfather's war was ancient history to her. The young always seemed to think in moral absolutes, but the world was rarely so black and white; the experiences of his own family had taught him that. His father had been a kind and decent man who fought bravely for South Vietnam, but his honor and courage counted for nothing when he found himself on the losing side and was punished for it.

Long needed to make arrangements for his time off, so they agreed to meet after lunch the next day at the Jade Emperor Pagoda. Long would show them around and take them to a couple of other places they might have missed, but he was already making mental notes for their trip to the country.

Long returned to the table, almost glowing from the call. Chau hoped it was the news she'd been longing for. "Was it about the job?" she enquired, trying not to sound excited.

"No," Long said and watched his wife's face drop faster than gravity allowed. He realized he had to be quick to sell his plan or face the consequences. "But the director wants me to send my resume to personnel," Long lied. "I don't want you to get your hopes up. That could as easily mean he wants it to vanish in paperwork as that he wants to examine my background and qualifications."

Chau clearly had processed only the first bit of the information. "But that's good, isn't it?"

"Well, as I said, it could be, but it could also be a means of letting me down gently."

Long hated lying to his wife. He loved her, and he recognized the nagging for what it was: concern for the family. He was the chief provider for three children. The reason Chau had no time for romance was that she had no time left. After managing their home, tending to the children and working part-time in a shop, she didn't have any energy left for nights of passion. Her guilty pleasures now were soap operas and subtitled Bollywood movies; the days of hot and heavy encounters at the back of the cinema were long gone.

Long had a choice: tell Chau another lie to cover his time with Tom and Emily, which would make things easier, or tell the truth and hope to convince her of its merits. He felt so guilty about the first untruth that he was compelled to be straight about the situation. "When I was with my mother in the park on Wednesday morning," Long started, "I met two Americans. One fought in the war, and the other was his granddaughter. I offered to help them while they're here."

"Oh, please don't tell me you're going to chase across the country. My father fought the Americans in Khe Sahn, and that is hundreds of kilometers away."

"No, I think he fought in this area and in Ap Trai Bí. He's looking for a particular village. I want to help him; he seems … troubled."

"My father said that the Americans are a strange people. He had never heard of a nation that would fight so hard, so far away from home. They would suffer hundreds of casualties to capture a hill and leave it the next day. It never made any sense to him; it probably never made any sense to the American soldiers, either."

Long was taken aback. Chau rarely talked about her father's war. He had been a captain in the NVA and, after the war, had elevated the family from fishermen on the northeast coast to wholesalers of fish in the south. Because of this significant rise in their social status, Chau and her brother had been the first generation in the family to go to university. This was important as prices were rising, and a good job was essential to stay ahead of the curve. The irony was not lost on Long that things had been so expensive under communist control.

The situation in the country had improved over the last couple of decades but not for Long. With hindsight, it might have been better for Chau to forge the great career. Her father was a war hero rather than a war criminal, and she would not have had her husband's struggle to climb the ladder of success. But Vietnam was still a traditional society, and when it came to having children, Chau saw it as her place to become the homemaker. She had her part-time job, but the bulk of the family's finances rested on Long's shoulders.

"Ap Trai Bí is just a couple of hours' drive away, but the villages are in the jungle, so we'll probably be gone three or four days," Long said as casually as he could before adding the sweetener he hoped would win her acceptance if not her approval. "They are paying me, of course; it's extra money."

"A few days of not being at your job, of not being with your family .... anyone would think you were looking forward to this," she scolded. She hadn't mentioned the money, but he could tell it softened the blow.

Long shrugged. "The American is looking for something; he needs to go where his spirit was broken. I think I can help him follow his path to the past ... if you agree."

Chau put down her spoon and looked at him with love in her eyes and the little smile he remembered from their first meetings. "You are a good man, that's why I married you. Many of my friends married brave veterans or men who were the sons of revolutionary heroes, and many of them turned out to be cruel or unfaithful or alcoholics. I knew that we would face problems, but I knew I would do that with a decent and honorable man. So, if you think you can help this broken American, then you should do it."

Long smiled his thanks.

"And I know the story about the director was bullshit," she added, wiping the smile from her face.

***

Tom and Emily had spent a near silent journey in the taxi to the Jade Emperor Pagoda. It was a sight that Emily had particularly wanted to see and one of their last stops before leaving the city. The noise and commotion of the streets were in contrast to the stillness in the taxi, where the distance between the two passengers had increased to become an unbreachable gulf. Each was feeling wounded and misunderstood and had no desire to be the first to try to reconcile. They pulled themselves together as the taxi came to a halt, and they saw Long's smiling face.

"Hello, hello!" he said enthusiastically.

Emily and Tom returned the warm greeting. "It's a beautiful Buddhist temple, isn't it?" Emily observed, anxious to let Long know she had done her homework.

"Actually, it's Taoist; the clue is the Chinese writing on the front - that's not Vietnamese," Long corrected.

"How are the religions different?" Tom asked.

"Well, I'm an engineer, not a priest, but Buddhism started in India; its followers strive to reach nirvana, sort of a state of perfection, through the teachings of the Buddha. Taoism started in China and emphasizes living in harmony according to the Tao. Vietnam has all kinds of religions because we are a crossroads to the world. We have Buddhist and Hindu temples, mosques, churches … all kinds."

"The Christians in Americans tend to want to convert people – to make others believe what they believe, like religion is a competition to see who has the best god," Emily commented.

"Ha! In Vietnam, we've been too busy fighting colonial powers and our neighbors to argue about which god is best. Besides, in this country, we often take a bit of one religion and mix it with another. Sometimes it's hard to see clear differences among them."

This impressed Emily. Her family was not religious, but all you had to do was turn on the TV to see religious leaders declare that to be a good Christian you had to believe one certain thing or face eternal damnation. The idea of a buffet view of religious beliefs appealed to her.

As they entered the temple, Tom was struck by the sweet smell of incense. The scented air seemed to complement the earthy colors inside. There, in all their metallic splendor, were several giant statues of mustachioed gods. One was standing on a slain dragon; another seemed to have killed a tiger. It was as foreign as it could possibly be from Tom's normal points of reference.

"Taoism is about simplicity and being at one with the natural flow of events. The key to its teachings is the concept of *wu-wei*, action without intent. This temple is for the Jade Emperor, one of the representations of the first god and one of the Three Pure Ones, the three great spirits of the Tao," Long explained in a reverential whisper.

To Tom and Emily, it sounded like a combination of 'Lord of the Rings' and an old martial arts movie. There was just no cultural framework for them to comprehend what Long was saying. This piqued Emily's interest and made Tom feel embarrassed by his ignorance. "You know, in all the time I spent in-country, I never once went to a place of worship,"

Tom whispered as he looked around in awe at the elaborate carvings.

Emily heard Tom's confession but suppressed a sigh of exasperation. What chance did the Americans ever have of fighting the communists if they never understood the people they were supposed to be fighting for? Instead, she contented herself by taking selfies with the rich interior behind her, carefully selecting which filter would be best to get the most online likes.

As the three of them took in their surroundings, a steady stream of locals filed in to pay their respects, light incense or pray. Despite the bustle, there was an air of purpose and calm. Even though this was exactly the sort of place Emily had been looking for, she felt disappointed. Admittedly, it was very different from anything else she had ever experienced, but why did she feel uneasy? Eastern mysticism had always appealed to her; she appreciated the zen-like calm of yoga and the meditation sessions. Why was this place not working on her? She looked over at her grandfather; maybe it was him, he was nothing but bad karma. Were his past sins tainting the atmosphere? Or maybe she was just frustrated by not being able to get a good signal on her phone so she could share her photos.

Tom had never thought he would find himself in a temple and was surprised to discover that it had a soothing effect on him. He allowed himself to sink into the atmosphere and turn his mind over to the things that were always uppermost: the loss of Elaine, the war and, now, the growing chasm between him and his granddaughter. Should he remember the ghosts of his past by making some kind of offering? Would it mean anything to them or to him if he did? He wondered if Elaine would understand any of this, and then he asked himself if this journey was doing more harm than good.

Long stood a respectful distance away and regarded the two of them. There was something wrong with the way they seemed to orbit each other but never overlap. Given a cultural background that emphasized respect for elders, Long did not understand Emily's apparent disregard for her grandfather. As for Tom, Long saw a man saddled with a terrible burden. Vietnam had tortured his humanity, and it was here that he would have to find a place to leave his burden if he wanted to find peace and heal his twisted soul. Americans were a contradiction to Long, so loud and confident in their movies and yet, on the few occasions he had met them, so lost and uneasy.

After a few more minutes in the temple, they left to visit the Reunification Palace. During the drive, Long peppered them with information, but neither responded beyond what was polite. The two barely acknowledged each other; the atmosphere was beyond cool.

At the palace, Emily, delighted to have found a good internet connection, photographed everything in apparently real time and looked to see what was new on her social media accounts, while her grandfather seemed to take a real interest in what had originally been known as Independence Palace. The grand building had been intended as a lavish home for the president of South Vietnam, but it became a symbol of the fall of Saigon in April of 1975, and the building remained frozen in time.

As the afternoon drew to a close, they decided to walk back to the hotel, now just a few streets away. As it came into view, they agreed plans for the following day and Long left them to head for home. When Tom realized they had stopped outside a bar, he turned to Emily, saying, "I think I'll stay here and have a beer."

"Fine, I'm going on to the hotel for a swim," Emily lied, the kernel of an idea now in full bloom. Back in the room, Emily checked her phone again. She had never intended to get bogged down in her grandfather's wartime past; it was time she got on with her own plans to tour Asia. So, with a reliable internet connection at the palace, not only had she been posting photos, but she had also been booking a flight. A friend had asked on Instagram if she was going to Angkor Wat – and now she was on her way!

She quickly wrote a note for her grandfather, packed her suitcase and headed down to reception. When she asked for a cab to the airport, the man at the desk apologized. There had been a traffic accident near the hotel and the road outside was closed, but if she walked over a block, there was a busy street where she could get one.

She thanked the receptionist, pulled out the handle on her suitcase with a satisfying snap and set off along the uneven sidewalk. Did she feel guilty about leaving her grandfather here on his own? Yes, but he had Long, and she was done with feeling depressed, embarrassed and disappointed. It was slow going, but she was making progress, moving forward with her original plans for the trip, unencumbered, at last, by her grandfather.

***

Tom had been pounding the beers for a while now. Propping up a bar stool, he indulged his feelings of abject failure in the war, then as a husband and father, and now as a grandfather. Was he shit at everything he did? He was fully absorbed in his own misery when two men sidled up to him.

"You American?" asked the first man in heavily accented English.

Tom regarded them both. They were ordinary looking Vietnamese, both smiling and nodding, clearly hoping that he was, indeed, American.

"Excuse me?" Tom said, his mind still trapped in self-pity.

"I want to know if you are American," said the man, a glint in his eye.

Tom squinted at the men a little suspiciously. "Why do you want to know?"

"You aren't Vietnamese, so I want to know where you come from."

"Oh, fine. I come from Chicago, so yeah, I'm American," Tom said, watching both men closely.

"You Americans, you killed my father!" the inquisitor shouted and produced a knife from his pocket.

In an instant, the world changed. Adrenaline flooded Tom's system and washed away the alcohol. Things had gone from slightly irritating to deadly serious in the space of seconds. The barman started shouting. Tom didn't need to understand the language to know he was alarmed, but the knifeman and his partner paid no heed to apparent warnings about calling the police. Somewhere in the back of his mind, Tom thought his assailant looked too young to be the son of a man from the 1970s, but that wasn't the point; his story might be false, but the knife was all too real, and Tom was focused on its six-inch blade. The man swung at Tom, who instinctively dodged the blow. Then, due either to age or alcohol, he stumbled and the knife swept through the thin air which Tom had occupied a fraction of a second earlier. Tom went down, falling in an undignified manner onto his butt, so that he was now sitting on the bar's sticky, linoleum-covered floor.

Tom watched in horror as the knife repositioned itself and hurtled toward his prone body. Just then a hand grabbed the limb that held the knife, twisted the arm and brought his wrist around, forcing him to drop the weapon. Tom tracked the limb up to its owner's face; it was Emily. She followed up with a punch to the gut and an elbow to the man's face, sending him reeling. The barman and one of the customers jumped on the stunned attacker and brought him down as his partner panicked and fled.

The knifeman screamed hysterically in Vietnamese. Whether he was genuinely angry about the death of his father, a common thug or a madman was unclear, but the customers pinned him to the ground while the barman called the police.

Emily looked down at her prone grandfather. She surveyed him anxiously, not knowing if he'd been hurt. "Grandpa, are you alright?" she asked, her voice trembling with emotion.

Tom nodded. "The only thing wounded is my dignity."

Relief flooded through her as Emily helped Tom to his feet. She had been dragging her case along the street where she had last seen him and recognized the bar as she passed it. When she heard the commotion, knowing her grandfather was probably inside, Emily dropped her case and ran to investigate.

"Tell me, where did you learn to fight like that?"

"Eric, my instructor in self-defense classes," she said before adding , "C'mon, let's get out of here. I didn't come to Vietnam to spend my time filling out police reports."

Astonishingly, her suitcase was exactly where she had abandoned it, and she grabbed it by the handle as they headed back to the hotel.

"Going somewhere?" Tom asked, now completely confused.

"Apparently not," was all Emily could manage as she reflected that it now looked as if, in addition to everything else, protecting her grandfather had been added to her list of responsibilities. This really was not the trip she had hoped for.

***

"Okay, men, here's the deal," de Bruin said to the soldiers in front of him. "After the attacks during Tet, the enemy has been beaten back. They are regrouping in a number of jungle locations, so we are returning by Hueys to the Ap

Trai Bí area where we found that deserted enemy position."

"You're kidding. If it was that important, why didn't we hang onto it?" whined Mo.

"Shut it, soldier," barked Zielinski.

De Bruin pretended he hadn't heard the private and continued. "As the location contained enough space to hold a company of VC, we are taking B, D and E companies into the area, plus a mortar team and air cover. The village where we will land has been designated a free-fire zone." Tom's squad was part of E for Echo company.

"Free-fire zone … but we all saw the families there," Ortiz whispered to Tom.

"Yeah, but where were all the young men, eh? Better to have permission to fire than not," Tom muttered back

"Gear up and take extra ammo; contact is expected to be heavy. We are going to tear them down before they have a chance to become too well entrenched. Company, dismissed," de Bruin ordered.

As the group was breaking up, Lieutenant Skoberne shouted over the noise, "Hold on a minute. Just before you head out, I am pleased to announce that Private Second Class Thomas Enrico Moretti is now Private First Class Thomas Enrico Moretti." The announcement was followed by cheers, applause and sarcastic comments. Eddie turned and slapped his buddy on the back by way of congratulations. Tom blushed and saluted the lieutenant.

"Sorry, Moretti, no time to celebrate or change your patch. You all heard the captain; it's time to lock and load."

The men checked their weapons, grabbed ammo, grenades and Claymores and headed to the waiting helicopters, a veritable swarm of giant metallic insects. The mechanical roar of the choppers reached a deafening crescendo as they heaved themselves into the air, their blades slicing through the early morning air. The men instinctively sat on their helmets. The floor looked solid, but it was made of aluminum and offered no protection from rifle fire. Better to sit on your helmet and put it on when you land rather than have it on your head and risk having your balls blown off from fire below.

The men were silent. The noise of the engines was too great to have any conversation, so they sat, lost in their thoughts, trying to keep fear from engulfing them. Tom felt sick but mustered a smile when the sergeant shot him a glance. It didn't matter how he felt, it was all about keeping yourself and your squadmates alive. Any hesitation in action or following orders could well result in death.

The choppers hung in the air like olive green dragonflies. The gunners stood by the side doors with their mounted miniguns, ready to unleash 4,000 rounds per minute. After fifteen minutes, the choppers began to descend toward the ubiquitous paddy fields with their crops of rice. As they came in to land, gunfire erupted from the farmers' houses. The VC had been waiting for them. The first three helicopters had landed and disgorged their troops, but a straggler was flying low and slow, the perfect target for an ambush.

Tom's chopper was about to land when several rounds of machine gunfire sizzled through the doorway and smashed through a window on the other side. The pilot lurched his controls, making them harder to hit as he flew erratically. The squad clung onto whatever they could, fearing they might be thrown out by the violently maneuvering Huey. The gunner began to pour on fire from his minigun, the muzzle erupting in bullets and creating a noise that rivaled the engine.

Tom was watching some of the men on the ground begin a maneuver to flank the machine gun posts when he saw a black-clad figure step out from a hooch and shoulder an RPG. "RPG!" Tom shouted uselessly; nobody could hear him over the uproar of battle. But the VC soldier wasn't aiming at their chopper, he was aiming for the one Captain de Bruin was in.

Tom watched as the metal missile streaked toward the landing Huey and tore off the tail section. The helicopter wobbled and smashed onto its side, sending razor-sharp chunks of propeller blade into the air. He continued to watch as Doc McCarrick, the medic, and the others got clear of the smoldering wreck. It seemed everyone had escaped without injury.

The troops on the ground were now taking the fight to the enemy, and the firing on the choppers diminished as the VC focused on the foot soldiers. The pilot of Tom's helicopter decided to land a little further away from the initial LZ, and Tom and his squad jumped down into the dark, dank waters of the paddy field. They were now out in the open with no cover.

"Fan out into a line and head toward the nearest hooch. And Powell, get ready to mow down anyone who isn't wearing olive green if you see movement," Zielinski ordered. The squad splashed forward, anxious to get out of the kill zone the VC had created. More helicopters buzzed around them in the air. Some waited patiently for the LZ to be cleared, while others circled, blasting away with their heavy machine guns and even rifle fire from the soldiers in the choppers.

Bullets screeched past Tom and he spun around. "Charlie at six o'clock," he shouted out to the rest of the men. Eddie immediately began firing his machine gun, a move that prevented the enemy from returning fire. The others took more careful aim, except for Mo, whose shotgun was useless at this range. He crouched down and trusted the others to do their jobs. The squad took out the three gunners who had been picking off unsuspecting soldiers as they disembarked from the helicopters, then they surveyed the tree line for more movement or muzzle flashes.

Tom could hear his own heavy breathing as the men dashed across the paddy field, their eyes darting around the field of battle. All thoughts were of taking down the enemy before it got a bearing on them. Suddenly, there was a burst of gunfire from a window facing the squad. The fire was full auto, fast and loud, but wild, the bullets missing them all. Everyone fell flat on their stomachs, their faces barely an inch above the foul smelling water. Tom brought his rifle to bear, and he and the other squad members fired a few rounds each in the direction of the window. The bark of an AK47 was the reply. Eddie opened up with the M60 and blasted the area below the window.

The power of his machine gun allowed his bullets to pass through the flimsy wall. There was no response. The men continued to move up as fast as they could, their clothes now drenched in the murky waters of the paddy field.

"Keep moving!" ordered Skoberne.

The men kept low but continued to squelch their way toward the relative safety of the nearest hut. Gunfire cracked around them. A plume of greasy black smoke rose from the horizontal Huey which was slowly catching fire. Another helicopter was leaving the area, smoke billowing out of its engine which had been hit by a burst of machine gun fire. The pilot was struggling to get it back to base before complete engine failure. Already there were fallen G.I.s bobbing in the water. Others were calling out in pain, but Tom and the squad didn't have time to think about the human cost of the battle; their main thought was to secure the hamlet from the insurgent enemy. No one wondered then if the death and destruction they caused simply created more insurgents.

At last, they were up against the wooden structure of the hooch, relieved to find cover. "Clear the house," shouted Skoberne.

This time it was Mo's turn to be point. In any close-quarters' encounters, the shotgun would take out a man with one round. They found the dead VC who had fired on them. He had taken two rounds to the chest, presumably from Eddie's fire. The rest of the dwelling was empty.

When the squad appeared out in the open again, figures could be seen running into the bush. The enemy was retreating. The more they could kill now, the fewer there would be to defend the hillfort nearby. Everyone opened up on the disappearing men. A water buffalo charged around between the two sides, out of its mind with terror caused by all the noise. Private Humby, a wild look in his eyes, riddled it with bullets. It let out a muffled cry of agony and staggered a few steps before its legs collapsed, and it fell to the ground. The poor beast rolled its eyes and moaned one last time before lying still, bright crimson blood gushing from the bullet wounds in its throat and side.

"Humby killed a cow," wailed Alabama. As a farmer, he understood that the loss could mean the end of a family's living.

"Looks like it's steak tonight," Humby shouted to his platoon. Tom couldn't help but smirk as a cheer rose from the rest of the men. Humby was crazy, a damaged individual, always looking to cause as much harm as he could, but he had a point. Fresh beef would be a vast improvement over the C-rations Tom had in his pack.

Skoberne brought them back to the fight when VC were spotted diving into the last house near the tree line. He signaled for one squad to flank them from the right while Tom and his squad were to flank the building from the left. Shots rang out, followed by a series of Vietnamese shouts and what sounded like screaming from inside the house. The soldiers fired off bursts of rifle fire to cover their progress toward the target. More AK fire rang out. A soldier screamed. Tom turned and saw that Corporal Ventura had taken a round to the forearm. The bullet had torn a chunk out of his arm, shattering his radius bone in the process.

"No fair! I just got back, it's not fair!" he screamed, clutching his bloody left arm.

One of the squad dragged him to cover and called for a medic. It would be the last time he saw action. After several painful rounds of surgery back in America, he would be left with a livid scar but near normal use of his left arm.

More shooting and screaming came from inside the hooch. Were the VC arguing or just excited about wounding an American? Tom and the others reached the side of the house. "They're going to have the doors covered. First man in is going to get zapped," Eddie said, cradling the M60.

"I've got an idea," Tom said, grabbing some detonating cord from his pack and sticking it in a rough joint of the hut's wooden wall. Skoberne nodded his approval, and Tom ducked around the corner to detonate the explosive. With a bang and a cloud of smoke, the primacord blasted a large hole in the side of the hut. The troops moved in. Two men were down on their hands and knees coughing from the fumes of the explosion. Blood was trickling from their ears, the sign of burst eardrums. The Americans didn't hesitate and shot them both dead.

Then they saw a third figure; it was that of a woman. She had been the one screaming. The men lowered their weapons. She was a farmer's wife and not a threat, but she continued to howl, tears pouring down her face. She kept pointing to where Zielinski was standing. The men looked at each other in confusion. Tom recognized the woman from the last time they were in the village. She was the one who had looked at him in disgust and hugged her baby closer because she feared what the American might do. But where was the baby?

Tom looked back to where they had entered. There, in a corner, was a charred cradle. As the realization took hold, Tom felt bile rise in his throat. What had they done? What had *he* done? His brainwave to blast their way into the hut had resulted in the death of a baby. The screaming they heard from the house had been an argument between the woman and the VC. She knew their presence in her home made her and her child a target. Now everything she feared had come to pass.

The sounds of the conflict outside drained away, leaving only the pitiful wails of the baby's mother. The men stood like statues, a cloud of shame hanging over their heads. Nobody wanted to move toward the cradle; to see what they had done would make it real. Tom found himself shaking as he stood rooted to the spot.

Eventually, Skoberne summoned up the courage to move and walked to where the baby's body lay. "Fuck," was all he could manage. Tears welled up in his eyes as he picked up the tiny body and carried it over to the grief-stricken mother, presenting it to her like the greatest treasure on earth. The woman took her dead daughter in her arms and let out an animal cry that ripped through every man in the room. As the men shuffled away from the scene of the crime, she singled out Tom and gave him a look full of anger and agony. She knew; she knew it was him.

Outside, Tom leaned against a corner of the house and vomited. He had killed a baby, an innocent, a life that had nothing to do with the geopolitics that had started this war.

A blameless infant was now dead because of his actions. Right then, he would have done anything to change places with the dead child.

Zielinski saw Tom crumble and walked over to put a reassuring hand on his shoulder. He was the sergeant, an experienced soldier supposedly inured to the horrors of war, but he was also a man, and he understood. Young Moretti, barely more than a child himself, had killed a baby. It was a burden he would carry forever but, right now, if Tom Moretti didn't get his mind back to the task at hand, he would likely be killed or get one of his squad killed. "Moretti, what you did, you did to save the lives of your squadmates. You didn't know there was a child behind that wall. You didn't choose that building for a firefight. That was Charlie, and if those commie bastards don't care about their own, there's not much we can do. The village was designated a free-fire zone. PFC Moretti, you took the correct course of action."

Tom knew the sergeant meant well, but his words rang hollow. Since when was the murder of a baby 'the correct course of action'? The war didn't make any sense anymore.

***

Shortly after their arrival in Vietnam, when Emily had gone for a swim one evening, Tom took the opportunity to call Eddie. After an eternity of ringing, he heard Eddie pick up and wheeze.

"Eddie, it's Tom."

"Give me … a minute, man … I'm just waking up."

"Oh, sorry. I forgot about the twelve-hour time difference. It's early evening here."

"Well, it's … early morning here … but that's okay … I was just … getting out of bed … So you got there … safe and sound … How's it going?"

It was a reasonable question. Tom began to assess everything that had happened since arriving. "Okay," he summarized.

"… Thanks for the insight …" Eddie replied sarcastically.

"I've been thinking about people I haven't thought about for decades … like Humby, remember him?"

"How could I forget that guy?"

"You know that after the war Humby worked in an abattoir, but that didn't scratch his itch, so he went on to kill an elderly woman. He was caught and eventually executed."

"Good … That was like putting … a rabid dog … out of its misery."

"I know, but was he always like that, or did the army make him that way? Sorry, coming back is dredging up a lot of stuff."

"Wasn't that … the point of … the whole exercise?"

"Yeah, but it's backfiring. It's my granddaughter; I think I've lost her. I showed her the park and the apartment block where we had that godawful firefight. Hell, we even met a woman who lived there, still lives there."

"No shit!" Eddie exclaimed, genuinely surprised.

"Yeah, her son offered to show us around, act as a guide."

"Now why would he do that?"

"Because it turns out the Vietnamese are nice people. We might have noticed that if we had stopped bombing and shooting them and actually talked to them."

"As I recall … they were shooting at us … too," Eddie said a little defensively.

"Anyway, I think I'm going to take him up on his offer. As for Emily … well, it's difficult in ways I hadn't expected. I guess I thought she'd be more understanding, but she can't get past what we did over here, and I haven't even got to the hard part yet."

"The village?"

"Yeah, the village. I'm going to ask Long, the Vietnamese guy from the park, to take me – and Emily if she decides to come with me. From there, I'm going up that trail. I have a promise to keep."

"You really want … to do that?"

"I have to."

"But if things are bad … with Emily now … what happened in … that village will only … make it worse."

"Oh, you think I don't know that? This new generation doesn't understand anything about us. The war is ancient history to them, and it's history they know nothing about, don't want to know about. "

"And what did we think … of the veterans … of World War I? … To us they were … just old men … who fought in a war … we knew nothing about … Look, just be honest … tell her the truth … and see what happens … She may surprise you."

"I'm dreading it, but it has to be done. I've spent my whole life refusing to think about what went down here. If this trip is going to mean anything, it requires total honesty."

"She comes from … good stock … Give her some time … Hell, it's taken you … this long to confront … your past … You can't expect anyone else to do better."

"I have to trust that our relationship is strong enough to weather the coming storm. Thanks for listening, man. I just wish you were here with me," Tom managed, his voice quivering with emotion.

***

Tom and Emily spent the morning buying equipment for the coming adventure. Tom had talked about seeing something of the 'countryside' when a better term would have been 'jungle'. Emily had not expected to sleep under canvas, but while she had her reservations, she found the idea both thrilling and scary. Even though she was deeply shaken by all that had happened since their arrival, she trusted her grandfather. As he gathered up equipment and provisions, she sat back and acquiesced to his obvious knowledge of what was required.

Meanwhile, Long was concerned. He had planned a visit to a small village, not some sort of jungle expedition. He knew he could get them to their destination, spend a couple of days with the locals, maybe see another village or two, but that was the extent of anything useful he could do. It soon became clear that Tom knew a lot more about what would be needed than he did. He seemed to assume that Long had some experience of the jungle whereas, in reality, he was just a city boy who was now wondering if his offer to help had got him into trouble.

Despite Emily's reservations and Long's concerns, they all met up as planned. Finding a driver to take them so far out of the city had been difficult, but Long knew someone who knew someone with relatives in the area, and he had agreed to drive them to the village where Tom had fought half a century ago.

After the incident in the bar, Tom made it clear to Emily that she did not have to accompany him on this side trip. He had warned her that if she thought the story about the damaged apartment was bad, there was worse to come. She had been tempted to make her excuses, but she had left it too late. The events of the previous evening reminded her that her grandfather was vulnerable, and now he was heading out into the Vietnamese countryside … jungle. She didn't want the responsibility, but she couldn't abandon him.

Emily knew her grandfather would not intentionally put her in harm's way, but after the fight in the bar, she now believed she might have something useful to contribute to the coming journey. Besides, she remembered telling Jessica that she wanted to find out what she could do above and beyond some predictable path. A jungle adventure might offer just that opportunity. It would certainly be something different, something outside her so-called comfort zone. She was worried about what else her grandfather's past would reveal, but she'd give it a shot and hope for the best.

Emily added her backpack to the equipment in the trunk and took a seat in the back of the car. If things became too boring or difficult, she could escape her surroundings by going on her phone. She'd heard that even the villages had wi-fi.

When they were settled inside, the driver tuned the radio to Asian pop, pulled out into the chaotic roads of the capital and headed north. He couldn't speak English and was happy to let Long play middleman and guide; he was there for the money. Tom and Emily didn't have much to say to each other, but they chatted amiably to Long. Tom was apprehensive about what lay ahead and not just for himself. He realized that things would get worse before they got better, but Emily had been warned ... not that any warning could absolve him of his sins or prepare his granddaughter for some hard truths. He just had to trust that there would be a way to bridge the growing chasm between them.

Emily gradually dropped out of the chatter and stared out of the window. Traffic was thinning as the bustle of the city turned into suburbs and then into farmland where water buffalo roamed the rice paddies. The well-maintained highway led to a poorly paved minor road that became little more than a dirt track. As the driver slowed to meet the conditions, excited children appeared and ran alongside the car, shouting and laughing and waving. Their enthusiasm was infectious and everyone but the driver waved back.

At the end of a three-hour drive, they came to a stop in what seemed to be the center of their destination, a village near Ap Trai Bí. Tom recognized it because it had not changed in any significant way since he'd last been here. He stepped out of the car and looked around to get his bearings and felt his stomach lurch as a profound sense of shame threatened to engulf him. He adjusted his baseball cap to repel the sharp glare of the sun and set off, moving swiftly over what felt like familiar ground. As he stepped off the path and into a paddy field to show them where he and his squadmates had hit the ground after leaving the chopper, the years fell away and Tom lost himself to the young soldier he had been. Emily and Long tried to stop him, but he shook them off as if in a trance.

"I wouldn't do that if I were you, " Long called out. "Around here they're still using buffalo and human manure to fertilize their crops."

Long's advice went unheard as long-suppressed memories flooded back, and Tom relived that terrible day, talking more to himself than to Emily and Long. The unusual activity in their quiet village attracted a little crowd of bemused locals, but Tom was oblivious. As his story progressed, Tom waded out of the paddy field and gestured to Long and Emily to follow him through the village. The flimsy huts made of wood and straw would have been rebuilt several times over since he had fought his way through them, but everything looked the same, including the last hut by the tree line, the scene of his greatest crime. As he described the appalling events, both Long and Emily found themselves caught up in Tom's passionate outpouring. It had stopped being a story and had turned into a confession.

By the time he had finished, all three of them were in tears. For Emily, it was the realization of her worst fears about her grandfather's crimes in Vietnam; for Tom, it was a full-frontal confrontation with his past; for Long, it was the very essence of all the tragedies his country had endured for over a century. What Tom didn't know was that the war with America came after long years of fighting with the French and then the Japanese. A century of war, a million crying mothers. In another life, Tom would never have killed a child, but in this life he had, and no amount of sorrow or regret could change that. Tom's life was cursed by the death of this child because he had been in the wrong place at the wrong time.

The villagers were curious and approached Long to ask why the crazy white man was running around in their paddy field. Exhausted by his efforts and deep in his recollections, Tom drifted over to where Long was in conversation. He turned to Tom, "The older people remember the day the American soldiers arrived in the village. They had argued with the Viet Cong because they knew that if their huts were used as firing positions, they would suffer and die. They didn't want the communists here any more than they wanted the Americans or the French or anyone else.

"They were terrified of the Americans. They had heard how they massacred populations, raped the women and burned houses and rice stores. As it turned out, they didn't do that the first time they came, and the second time, they fought the battle but moved on. No massacre, no rapes, no burning. They thought themselves lucky."

"Lucky?" Tom said, horrified. "How shit were things if that was considered lucky?"

Long shrugged. Emily was stunned and speechless.

"What happened to the mother?" Tom felt compelled to ask.

Long checked again with the villagers. "They remember that she left shortly afterward; she was still clutching her baby. They don't know where she went." Then Long added, "Any woman on her own was vulnerable, especially to men with guns. She could have joined the Viet Cong, lots of women did, or she could have ended up as a bar hostess in Saigon. Both fates are equally likely."

Tom remembered the look on the woman's face; it was a look that reflected all-consuming hate, and at that moment he knew she had joined the VC. She was looking for revenge.

While Tom was turning everything over in his mind, Emily was grappling with her phone. She was overwhelmed by the revelations and desperately needed to share her horror, but the signal was weak. She swore under her breath and then sighed with resignation. Whether she liked it or not, she had committed herself to this, all of this, including the shocking account of her grandfather's war crimes. If he was determined to see this through, so was she. If this was some kind of test, she wanted to be up for the challenge. There was no going back for either of them.

Long broke into their thoughts. "The villagers are inviting us to stay. No American has come here since the war, and they feel honored that you have traveled so far to re-visit your past ... because it is, of course, their past, too."

While he was talking, the villagers started to crowd around Tom and Emily, and some of the women began touching Emily's blonde hair. She kept hearing, "*Ngôi sao điện ảnh*" over and over again.

"Sorry," Long apologized. "These are poor village folk. I doubt they've ever seen a white woman with blonde hair before."

"What are they saying?" Emily asked.

"You mean, '*ngôi sao điện ảnh*'?"

"Yes."

Long smiled. "It means 'movie star'." Emily blushed and submitted to the caresses.

A pig was slaughtered in honor of the guests that had come to their tiny hamlet, and that night everyone feasted. They sat around the fire and shared stories as well as steaming bowls of sticky rice balls with boiled vegetables and pork. The food was delicious and the fire cast a warm glow over the proceedings. So, too, did the rice wine. Tom knew it had a kick when he felt it burn all the way down.

When he had come to his senses after wading in the paddy field, Tom had asked if he could wash and change his clothes. Now he was asking Long how they could repay the villagers for their many kindnesses. Long replied that they were unlikely to accept any payment as it would offend their sense of hospitality; the visitors had novelty value, especially as they had come such a long way. Besides, Tom was clearly an 'elder', and the Vietnamese almost venerated their elders, particularly one who represented a link to the history of the village. Tom was a piece of living history and was held in high regard.

Emily had forgotten about an internet connection and had settled down to try some of the local beer with her meal. "This pork is so full of flavor. I've noticed a lot of pigs in the countryside," Emily commented.

"Yes, we Vietnamese love pork. I've never eaten a pig I didn't like," Long joked.

Now that he had calmed down and was surveying his hosts, Tom noticed the same pattern as when he was last here: the majority of the population was either old or very young, with few people in the middle. Back in '68, it was because of the war, but it couldn't be the same this time around. "Where are all the young adults?" Tom asked, directing his question to Long.

"They all go to the city for work. Farmers are poor, so young people want to go where there are paying jobs. Even the lowliest work pays better than farming, especially if they can get factory jobs. But they all return to their home villages during Tet and other holidays. Meanwhile, everyone keeps in touch with their phones. We have the internet pretty much everywhere in Vietnam; it's not always reliable in the countryside, but it's getting better."

Long was kept busy with all the translating, but he was enjoying himself. On the surface, he had little in common with these poor and illiterate farmers, but they were genuine and hospitable. He was an urban dweller with an engineering degree, but he knew his own family was only a few generations on from rural life. Just as Tom was a link to the recent history of the village, Long felt an association to his past through these villagers. I guess we're all connected in one way or another, Long mused, his thoughts turning to the next day.

Someone had mentioned that Tom might want to visit a nearby hill, something Tom confirmed. This caused Long some anxiety. The war might have happened a lifetime ago, but people were still dying from unexploded bombs and mines, and Tom wanted to visit a place which was known to have seen combat. Were there any unseen dangers lurking just below the soil? Who knew?

Long realized that he was now completely out of his depth. They were going to need a local guide, someone who knew the area and any potential dangers from unexploded ordinance or possibly even tigers. He wasn't entirely sure there were tigers in this part of Vietnam, but his childhood fear of being alone in the jungle and coming face-to-face with a wild animal surfaced once again.

Much as Tom was enjoying the hospitality of villagers who had good reasons to be other than welcoming, his mind kept drifting to the plans he had made. Despite the fear and dread that haunted him, there were places he needed to visit: The first had been the park, where he had been met with warmth and consideration by Long and his mother. The second was this village, the scene of his most terrible crime, a place marked back then by his nation's policies of wanton destruction, but where today he was met, once again, with friendliness and hospitality, rather than the hostility he had expected and believed he deserved. The nearby hill was the third place. It had seen fierce fighting, and he wondered if unexploded ordnance still lurked. Would he be endangering them all in this selfish pursuit? A fourth destination was also on his mind, but much as he felt compelled to return there, he knew the dangers would be even greater. That last stop was one he might have to undertake alone.

Tom glanced over at Emily. It was the first time on the trip he had seen her so animated; his granddaughter seemed to have come alive. They had been lucky to meet Long, an English-speaking university graduate and a superb guide, but there was more to Vietnam than urban life. Now they were meeting the people of the countryside and villages and had time to immerse themselves in their surroundings. This was exactly what Emily had hoped to find on her travels, but she could never have guessed that it was her grandfather who would make it possible. She took photos and video footage of some of the village elders holding the gathering in rapt attention as they told their stories. The fact that she couldn't understand a word of any of it seemed only to make the experience more memorable.

With conversation almost impossible, Emily took out her phone to play some music, a language everyone could understand. The villagers nodded approvingly and seemed to assume that a woman who looked like a movie star must be a singer as well. Emily tried but couldn't ignore the unmistakable gestures that indicated they wanted her to sing. She grimaced and quickly found something by Taylor Swift. When 'Ready for it?' blared out, she proceeded to half-sing and half-mime her way through a track that went on for far longer than she remembered. Her performance ended to wild applause, and Emily had to admit that having an uncritical audience had greatly enhanced her limited musical talents.

But because of his age and his history with them, it was Tom who was the star of the evening. Stories from the war evolved to those reflecting a lighter mood and went on to generate others that made everyone laugh. The villagers had not rejected Tom; they had not ignored or even questioned him. How was it possible that a man who had brought disaster to their lives could be accepted so readily? Was joy the antidote to inhumanity? However devastating events, people sought normality and clung to it as a way of surviving.

As the evening wore on, several villagers invited the visitors to bed down on sleeping mats in their huts. Long accepted readily, but Tom and Emily excused themselves and made use of a tent. For Tom, it was the best night's sleep he'd had since Elaine had been diagnosed with cancer.

***

Tom squatted down, his M16 cradled in his arms. Over and over again, his mind still played the death of the baby even as he tried to concentrate on what Lieutenant Skoberne was telling the platoon.

"Alright, men, that was the hottest LZ I've ever been in. Delta Company was hit the worst, but it's good to see most of the rest of us made it through the village with minimal casualties. Now we need to move to that fixed position on the hill. We are going to approach from three directions so the enemy can't concentrate on any one company. Also, before our assault, the mortars are going to lay down some smoke so it doesn't turn into a kill zone. Any questions?"

There was silence.

"Okay then, let's move out."

The platoon started to fan out under the jungle canopy, moving silently through the dense foliage. While his squadmates scanned every bush and clump of vegetation for a possible ambush, Tom followed, still lost in mental anguish. Ortiz let go of a branch he was holding as he passed, and it whipped into Tom's face. "Ow," he said, reacting more to the surprise than the pain.

Ortiz spun around and glared at Tom, putting his index finger to his lips. Tom nodded in understanding and signed an apology. He had to get back in the game or risk jeopardizing everyone in the squad. He didn't mind dying himself; in fact, right now, he felt he deserved it, but he didn't want to let the squad down by failing to do his bit. Every man needed every other to stay alive.

The soldiers passed through the jungle like green ghosts, working at a methodical and steady pace, their hunched forms creating minimal profiles. When visibility was just a few feet ahead, when paths were likely to be booby-trapped, each man had to be aware of the man in front at the same time as their eyes darted to and fro, looking for any movement, their rifles primed and ready for action. The only sounds were those coming from the jungle: the rush of the river, the calls of exotic birds and the whoops of passing monkeys. Any noise seemed painfully loud as the soldiers strained to hear anything that didn't belong. The track brought them to the river, lower than before when the rains had swelled it. This time it would be easier to wade across. Once over this barrier, they knew they were close.

Suddenly, about fifty feet away, a man popped out of the ground and fired at point blank range. The targeted soldier was dead before he hit the ground. Then the VC turned his weapon on another soldier who was only now reacting. The VC fired as the G.I. brought his rifle to bear. More shots rang out and a second American was dead before he had time to pull his trigger. By now all the soldiers were aiming at the VC, and a hail of gunfire ripped through his body before he collapsed back into the tunnel.

They cried out for a medic, but both soldiers were already dead. Skoberne approached the entrance to the tunnel where he pulled out his 45 and a flashlight and almost dived into the hole. It was small and damp and claustrophobic. Skoberne snapped the light from one side of the tunnel to the other, ready to blast anything there, but apart from the VC corpse, the tunnel was empty. He squirmed his way out and gestured for the men to gather around. There was a blast of radio chatter from Ortiz's field radio as he quickly gave an update to Captain de Bruin. Meanwhile, Skoberne turned to his men. "Okay, we are going to push on, but Jones and Jones," he said, pointing to

Alabama and Mo, "will go down the tunnel. Who knows, maybe they can kill all the dinks before we get to the top."

Mo and Alabama stripped off their bulky helmets and unnecessary equipment, and Skoberne handed Alabama his Browning semi-automatic pistol. With the pistol in his right hand and a k-bar in his left, Alabama was the first to enter. Mo was right behind him with his shotgun at the ready. Once past the entrance, the tunnel enveloped them in its total darkness. Mo knew Alabama was right in front of him and that, if he reached out, he could touch him, but he couldn't see any part of his squadmate. The only sounds were coming from the faint scrabbling of their feet on loose dirt and their heavy, shallow breathing as they crept along in a direction that took them into the hill.

Outside, the rest of the squad continued picking its way through the roots and vines. The shooting had focused Tom's mind like nothing else. He was ready for action, ready to fight again.

Eddie wordlessly pointed out a massive trail of biting red ants, and the men were careful to avoid disrupting the insect convoy for fear of painful bites. A few minutes later, Skoberne was on Ortiz's radio when the call came in that the mortars were set up and ready to fire. Once the smoke bombs were deployed, the men started making their way up the hill. Gunshots rang out as the VC began to blind fire, and Tom, like the others, brought all his senses to bear on the coming fight.

Down in the tomb-like tunnel, the opening volleys of the battle above were muted, like distant thunder. Alabama pushed forward, certain that Mo was right behind him and that he would have his back. Alabama could tell by the change of the air on his face that he had moved into a larger space, some kind of bunker or maybe just a passing space, impossible to tell in the pitch black. Then he heard it. Breathing, breathing near him. He hadn't heard Mo's breath behind him, so this meant someone else was there in the dark. Still holding his k-bar, he reached out his first two fingers to feel around for the man, while his other senses searched frantically for clues. It was his nose that alerted him to the smell. There was a musky scent in the air, the other man's body odor. He could be only inches away.

Alabama groped around on the ground until his fingers felt something firm. Too soft for a root, it must be a leg. At that moment, a knee smashed into his nose. Alabama knew that if he could see, his sight would be blurry from the impact. Sweaty hands grabbed at his right forearm and managed to wrestle his gun from his hand. He swung his knife through what turned out to be thin air and felt it embed in the tunnel wall. Now he felt a sharp pain in his right arm. Was the VC biting him?

"Help me," hissed Alabama, but Mo could see nothing, and if he fired his shotgun at this range, he was going to pepper Alabama even if he could see his target. All he could do was anxiously await the outcome.

Alabama wrestled the man off his arm, but he had no weapon; his gun was somewhere on the ground, and his k-bar was stuck uselessly in the wall. The other man flailed frantically in the dark and was now on top of him. He felt the guerilla pressing down with all his might on his neck, trying to stop the flow of blood to his brain by jamming down hard on his carotid artery. This was bad. If Alabama didn't do something in the next few seconds, he would black out and die under the knee of his attacker. He tried to shift his weight from under the man, but his assailant had a fierce hold on him and there was little room for maneuver. He tried to punch the man, but his blows landed weakly.

"You okay, man?" Mo breathed, genuinely concerned for his buddy. He could hear grunts and scuffling but didn't know what was going on just feet from him. Some might regard Alabama as a white devil but, in reality, he was just a dirt-poor farmer who had about as much chance to better himself as the average black man. Alabama, in socio-political terms, was black; he just didn't know it. Mo hefted his shotgun. If he didn't hear anything from his squadmate in the next few seconds, he might as well blast away. Better to kill a commie bastard before the bastard killed him - and it would be fitting revenge for Alabama.

Back on the ground, Alabama knew that time was running out. Unless he could get some sort of weapon, the VC would be the death of him. His hands thrashed about as he searched for anything he could use as a weapon - and then his right hand banged against something hard in the wall, his k-bar. He gripped it tightly and, summoning all his strength, wrenched it out of the wall. Then he turned the knife 180 degrees and smashed it into the side of his attacker who screamed in pain. With his left hand, Alabama jammed his balled fist into the man's mouth to stifle the cry. He yanked the knife out of the man's side and felt warm blood splash onto his crotch. He jabbed it back in again and again and again until the VC stopped struggling and fell limp on top of him.

"Alabama, if you can hear me, say something, or I'm going to fire my cannon at everything in front of me," whispered Mo.

Alabama let out a controlled gasp. "No, don't. I'm okay," was all he could manage as he gulped down lungfuls of stale air, his chest heaving up and down after the exertions of the hand-to-hand combat. That had been close, real close.

"I need to switch the flashlight on, just for a few seconds. I have to find my gun," Alabama murmured, breathing heavily.

"You do that, you give away our position to anyone in this tunnel, and we've got no cover," Mo warned.

"And between him screaming, and the battle going on above us, I reckon it doesn't matter. Now shut your eyes so at least *you* don't lose your night vision."

Mo snapped his eyes shut. Alabama switched on the light and saw the gun lying propped up against one wall of what turned out to be a little room. The dead guerilla was lying not far away, face down on the floor; blood caked his torso and was pooling around him. When Alabama glanced down for a quick look at his arm, he saw the bite marks from the fight. They were red and bleeding and would probably become infected, but right now, that was the least of his worries. The light also revealed a horror show of dark blood smeared across his chest, lower torso, legs and arms.

Alabama used his shirt tail to wipe some of it from his hands to stop them being slippery. Then he quickly glanced down the tunnel to see it curve away about fifty yards further up. Nobody was there. He picked up his gun and snapped off the flashlight.

Overhead, the Americans scurried forward toward the brow of the hill. Men began to fall with the loud sound of percussion. "Mines!" Zielinski shouted. The sides of the hill had been reinforced with pit traps filled with punji sticks and toe-popper mines. These were designed to maim rather than kill, to slow down any assault, and they were working.

Hidden machine gun positions dug into the sides of the hill began to fire, and everything came alive with the roar of KPV heavy machine guns, the bark of AKs and the crack of rifle fire. Eddie blasted away with his M60 while other infantrymen returned fire with their M16s.

Many of the logs and ridges the Americans sought for cover were booby-trapped, and the men were reduced to tossing smoke grenades to get some kind of relief from the withering fire. Everyone hugged the ground as the assault faltered. It was a base human instinct to resist the angry hornet's nest of bullets and fire emanating from the hill.

Occasionally a VC appeared from apparently nowhere and fired off a clip of ammunition at any Americans nearby. He was quickly cut down, and the hole where he had appeared was fragged to kill any lurking enemy soldiers. The barking of gunfire accompanied the louder crump of detonating grenades as bullets whizzed overhead. Something needed to be done. Tom looked around; everyone was waiting for someone else to do something.

As the smoke cleared, specialist Ramirez saw his opportunity. He brought his thumper to bear and aimed the grenade launcher at one of the hidden fire points. He fired the 40mm grenade into the enemy where it detonated with a deep, satisfying thud. The machine gun fell silent. There was cheering as the enemy was silenced.

"Keep moving," ordered Skoberne, seeing this as a chance to reclaim the initiative. "We stay here, we die. This is a kill zone and we're sitting ducks," he added, grabbing a nearby private by the collar of his flak jacket and dragging him forward.

The men began to get into a rhythm. Covering fire and move, push forward and then lay down suppressing fire. Move and shoot, move and shoot. Soldiers were still falling, some wounded, some dead, but momentum was returning to the attack. Tom saw Doc McCarrick run to a soldier who had taken a bullet to the chest. He was getting his bandages out when a second bullet went through the man's left eye. Even though he was fifty yards from the doctor, Tom could see the look of helplessness and frustration on his face. Tom knew exactly how he felt.

The men had begun to zero in on the enemy fire points and were dropping them as quickly as the enemy tried to reinforce them. The Americans were getting closer and closer to the ridgeline. Skoberne got on the radio. The delay in their early attack meant they needed more smoke from the mortar team.

Humby let out a primal scream and was first over the ridgeline. Tom was close behind. Smoke swirled all around him, and bullets sizzled past him as he jumped over the crest of the hill. He hit the ground and crawled through the dirt, rifle in hand. The other members of the squad followed him. Eddie set up his pig and waited to cover his squadmates when the protective smoke screen cleared.

Men shouted, their voices muted in the churning gray cloud. Some were Americans, others were not. The enemy was close. Through the whirling mist, Tom saw the head and shoulders of a man appear from a slit trench, about ten feet to his three o'clock. He brought his rifle to his shoulder and fired a burst of three shots, taking the enemy soldier out before he'd even seen Tom. Zielinski moved past him in a crouch and paused to pat Tom on the shoulder as a sign of approval.

The enveloping smoke was starting to thin, leaving the Americans out in the open. The Vietnamese could now stop firing wildly at imagined shadows and direct their volleys with deadly accuracy. Ramirez took another shot with his m79 and blew two Vietnamese soldiers into a red mist, but he screamed as bullets ripped into his side and hip. He dropped to the ground, clutching his wounds.

The firefight on top of the hill was fierce, and the G.I.s had no cover against an entrenched enemy firing from the safety of bunkers and slit trenches. "Find cover under the ridgeline," bellowed Skoberne. Soldiers started to retreat back to the side of the hill. It was more than a little ironic that the slope, infested with traps and mines, was at that moment considered a sanctuary for the Americans.

Tom scrambled over to Ramirez. "Can you walk?" Tom asked.

Ramirez shook his head. Without thinking, Tom shouldered his rifle, grabbed Ramirez by his flak jacket and began to drag him off the top of the hill. Ramirez cried out in pain.

"Sorry," Tom muttered.

"Just go! Get me out of here," Ramirez cried.

Bullets zipped by the two soldiers, some kicking up dirt. As Tom grappled Ramirez out of the kill zone, Zielinski appeared to help Tom maneuver the moaning Ramirez below the crest of the hill and the safety of temporary cover. Doc McCarrick ran to Ramirez, saying to Tom, "Good work, son." In his early forties, Doc was just about old enough to be the father of most of the men, and his thinning hair, covered by his helmet, made him look even older. As Doc got to work, Tom looked down at his wounded squadmate. "Thanks, man," Ramirez said, looking back at Tom. Ramirez would be shipped back home and, while he would survive his wounds, his pelvis was shattered. He would need a cane for the rest of his life.

To Mo and Alabama, the battle above them sounded strangely distant and muted. They knew they had to keep going. If they could distract the VC, it might give their brothers-in-arms the breathing space they needed. When they came to the end of the tunnel, they found a basic trap door above them. Cracks in the cover revealed a dim light source coming from above; it must be a lantern. Alabama put away his k-bar and gripped the Browning tightly in his hand. He was going to fling open the door with his left hand

and sweep the room with his gun in his right in case there was a waiting party. As Alabama wrenched open the cover, he scanned the room for enemy activity and missed seeing something metallic by his head. The grenade detonated at point-blank range, spraying his blood, brains and bone all over the tunnel entrance, killing him instantly.

Mo fell backward, partly from the blast and partly from the shock of seeing Alabama's bloody remains collapse back into the tunnel. He stared wide-eyed at the gory mess that only moments earlier had been his friend. He simply couldn't believe what he was seeing and covered his mouth as an involuntary cry tried to break out. Then he heard voices. The detonation had alerted the defenders that somebody had fallen prey to their booby trap.

Mo quickly wiped away the tears that were forming and slunk back into the tunnel, positioning himself so that he couldn't be seen from above. If anyone tried to come down, he would tear them to pieces with his Stevens Model 77E shotgun. The voices grew louder; Mo could tell they were almost on top of him. As more light poured down the mouth of the tunnel, he took a step back to guarantee he would be lost in the shadows.

Mo had no idea what was being said but, judging by the number of voices, three men were surveying the situation and chuckling over the fate of the dead soldier. Their cheeriness provoked a visceral response in Mo. How could those dirty gook bastards find the death of his friend funny? He gripped his weapon a little tighter and tensed himself for an attack. As the VC continued their conversation, the tone was changing from jokiness to disagreement. Mo presumed they were arguing about who would get the difficult job of clearing away the body and cleaning up the mess.

After a few minutes of debate, Mo saw someone drop down eight or nine feet in front of him. The man had his back to Mo as he looked up and continued to chatter with his comrades above. He began to manhandle Alabama's body and groaned, either through disgust or the effort of moving the dead weight, his sandals slipping in the sticky, pooling blood. There was more excited chatter, accompanied by a few laughs.

Mo edged forward. He needed to be as close to the mouth of the tunnel as possible so that after he took down the first man, he could, hopefully, zap the others before they knew what hit them. The man linked his arms around Alabama's chest and called to the others for assistance. When Mo saw the hands of the other men reach down to help heave the corpse, he knew that was his moment.

With a resounding bang, the buckshot from his 12 gauge cartridge tore through the man's back and shredded his organs as the balls of metal, traveling at the speed of sound, punctured most of his major organs. He collapsed backward as Mo pumped the shotgun and chambered his next round. The two other Vietnamese were caught completely by surprise. When they peered down into the tunnel, Mo took aim and, with a snarl of anger, fired at point-blank range into one of the men's faces, killing him instantly. The third man ducked out of view.

Mo stood up and pumped another round into his weapon, moving to get a better view of the space above him. The third man was stumbling toward his AK47, propped against the wall. Mo fumbled the shot, just clipping the man but blasting the AK across the room. The VC frantically changed direction to grab another rifle. Mo quickly adjusted his aim, loaded another round and fired again, this time peppering the man's legs with buckshot. The VC fell to the ground with a cry. Mo spied the pistol Alabama had been using, lying at his feet. He quickly picked it up and hoisted himself out of the tunnel to bear down on the wounded VC, who was slowly crawling toward a gun.

Holding his shotgun in his left hand, Mo swung the butt of it at the man's head, using it as if it were a club. The soldier grunted in pain. Mo kicked the man over so that he was lying on his back and aimed the Browning at the VC soldier's chest. The men locked eyes. Two men, separated by race, language, culture and ideology glared at each other. Each one knew exactly what the other was thinking. Mo knew that the VC fighter was scared and didn't want to die; the VC fighter looked into the eyes of the black American, saw only cold fury and knew he wanted revenge. They had nothing in common, but right now, they had everything in common.

"Not so funny now, is it, motherfucker?" Mo snarled and fired four rounds into the man's chest. The VC weren't human, they were just gooks.

Nobody came to see what the noise was about; the gun battle above ground seemed to be keeping everyone else busy. Mo walked past the dead VC to the body of Alabama and winced. Half his head was missing, and what was left hung limply from his neck. Mo would ensure that his body was retrieved at the end of the battle, and a folded flag would be sent to Robert 'Alabama' Jones's family. They would mourn the loss of their nineteen-year-old boy for years to come.

But that was in the future. Right now, Mo had a mission. He methodically reloaded his Stevens Model 77E and tucked Lieutenant Skoberne's pistol into his belt at the small of his back. He was determined to wreak a bloody path of destruction through this series of bunkers to avenge his buddy.

While Mo was battling through the Viet Cong subterranean complex, Lieutenant Skoberne was calling in an airstrike on the field radio, now on Ortiz's back. A hissing voice stated that the ETA for the two Douglas A-1E Skyraiders was six minutes.

The soldiers fired sporadically to keep enemy heads down and ensure that they had to be totally preoccupied with manning their defenses. The minutes felt like hours. All the adrenaline meant Tom was bursting for a whizz, so he rolled over and quickly peed to one side.

"Careful, Moretti!" complained Private Gorny.

"Hey, I gotta go."

Eddie chuckled and continued to scan the ridgeline for any enemy movement when they all heard what sounded like a helicopter. As the noise got louder, they realized the engines were running too fast for a chopper. It was more of a drone. The Skyraiders had arrived. In the jet age, they were propeller-driven anachronisms but, because they could fly low and slow, they were perfect for bombing runs to assist ground troops close to the target. The roar of the propellers echoed off the treetops and nearby mountain ridge as they honed in, each one of these great mechanical birds carrying a large, streamlined pod under its fuselage. As they dived down, the VC fired, but the pilots had chosen a steep angle, and the enemy didn't have time to get their big guns in position.

Silently, the pods were released, and the troops craned their heads to watch them topple end-over-end. When they hit their target, they did so with a bright flash and an explosion of napalm. The petroleum jelly ignited on impact, turning the top of the hill into a raging inferno. The Americans instinctively hugged the ground as burning air rushed past them; it was as if a giant oven door had opened in their faces. The soldiers cheered.

"Those planes are almost as old as me. They were everywhere back in Korea, and it's kind of nice for them to have my back again," Zielinski observed, seemingly oblivious to the raging chemical firestorm going on just above him. Oily black clouds billowed into the air; the sound of crackling fire was laced with screams of agony from the men caught in the searing furnace. Minutes passed as the G.I.s watched the napalm do its work for them. When the flames began to subside, the jungle floor appeared to get up and move as the three companies of Americans began to charge up the hill again. The enemy company was surrounded. It had nowhere to run and no option but to fight to the last man.

Tom and Eddie moved swiftly up the slope, praying they wouldn't disturb another commie trap. When they burst over the side of the hill this time, what they saw was a scene from hell. The trench works were a smoldering ruin, and blackened corpses lay in macabre positions. Pools of napalm still burned hot and smoke poured off everything organic.

Shots rang out. Some of the enemy soldiers had managed to find cover and escape the napalm firestorm. Eddie opened up with his heavy machine gun and killed two in a burst of gunfire. Tom had seen shooting coming from one of the slit trenches and sprinted toward its lip to hurl a grenade with the force of a major league pitcher. Kill or be killed, do or die. The detonation was accompanied by a scream. Tom jumped into the ditch and saw a dead soldier lying on his front, the grenade having torn chunks out of his back. Zielinski was right behind him, and the rest of the squad followed. Tom moved along the trenchworks, checking his corners and stepping over burning debris and bodies. A crazed enemy soldier came screaming around the bend, a bayonet fixed on the end of his rifle. Tom and Zielinski both fired a couple of rounds into the man who staggered and fell dead to the ground.

Tom looked around. The whole area was now swarming with American soldiers. It looked like they had taken the hill and killed an enemy company. Eddie took out a cigarette and lit it on a burning piece of wood sticking out of the mud. Tom stared at him and shook his head as if to say he thought Eddie a lost cause. Eddie just grinned his big, cheeky grin.

The squad moved on and came to the mouth of a dugout where a badly burned VC was propped up against the doorway. His left arm and shoulder were black, two of the fingers on his left hand were missing, and a chunk of his hair had burnt off. He lay there moaning, so overcome by agony that he was oblivious to the American soldiers.

Zielinski nudged Tom and gave him a nod; he wanted Tom to kill him. Tom looked down at the clothes that were still smoldering from the napalm attack. If there was a hell, he was already there. Tom didn't see a wounded dink; what he saw was a wounded man, a human being who had fought hard but was thwarted by a weapon he could barely conceive. Was Zielinski being cold-blooded or humane? Did he even know the difference anymore? Tom had seen and caused enough death for one day, in fact for a lifetime … hell, for ten lifetimes! Tom shouldered his rifle and reached for his canteen. It wasn't much, but maybe he could give this poor man some respite.

"What the hell are you doing?" Zielinski angrily asked and raised his M16, his finger reaching for the trigger.

Just then a shot rang out from inside the bunker, and the wounded man slumped over, dead. The gunshot made everyone jump, and weapons were aimed at the doorway, where a figure from a horror movie blinked as he stepped into the sunlight. It was Mo. His flack jacket, arms and face were covered in blood, and his eyes contained an inferno to match the napalm firestorm. As he stepped forward, he worked the pump of his shotgun, and a spent green cartridge spiraled to the ground. The men lowered their rifles. Everyone was relieved to see him even as they tried to look behind him. Mo stood silent and shook his head, slowly and deliberately. It was Zielinski who asked the question on everyone's lips, "Where's Alabama?"

"Sir, the remains of Private Robert Jones are in a tunnel. Since his demise, I have fought my way through these dugouts to get above ground." The only part of the sentence that wasn't said with dripping insubordination was the part where Mo voiced Alabama's rank and name.

Zielinski nodded. "Moretti, help Mo bring Private Jones's body topside."

Tom nodded and ducked into the bunker. It took five minutes for Mo to find the place where Alabama lay. Tom shut his eyes in revulsion. Alabama's head was so badly mangled, he wouldn't have been able to identify him, but his build and uniform confirmed that this was their dead squadmate and friend. Who could ever have predicted that a poor southern farmer would die in a VC tunnel halfway around the world. The two men stood silently staring at the body as tears trickled down Mo's cheeks. Tom put his arm around Mo's shoulders and felt a lump in his throat that made breathing almost impossible. When would this nightmare end and at what cost thought Tom. And who would be next?

***

Tom woke up and groaned. It was the morning after the night before. His mouth felt like the cat's litter tray and, even with his glasses, it took time to focus. His head throbbed, and as he moved to get up, a wave of nausea washed over him. He stopped and leaned on one elbow, then looked over at Emily who was starting to stir.

Emily felt a little rough around the edges as she came to her senses. She'd had a restless night. The combination of heat, humidity and mosquitoes were something she'd never get used to. How had her grandfather endured it over so many long weeks and months? She stretched, looked around and saw his weak smile. She nodded and looked away as she began to recall something of the night's dark dreams. Maybe there was some sort of resonance with the crimes perpetrated in this village she mused. But that was silly; it wasn't like the locals thought tortured souls haunted their huts.

The sun was high in the sky when Long awoke much later. It turned out that country air and the tranquillity of this sleepy little hamlet had a soporific effect on him. When he stepped out of the hut, he was amused to see Emily and Tom moving around the village, a crowd of boisterous children surrounding them, each one vying to attract the attention of the visitors. The Americans looked so out of place, even more than he did.

Emily hadn't anticipated that her nursing education might be useful, but it had kicked in as a reflex. When the villagers had gathered last night, she couldn't help but notice some of the older generation with injuries that must have come from the time of the war. In addition, there were many ailments and disorders that could – should - be treated now. She knew that minor conditions, if treated early, could be cured before they became serious. What sort of medical facilities did they have? She found Long and asked.

Long explained that while most villages had at least rudimentary schools, they lacked provisions for health care. Anything serious would have to be treated in the largest nearby town where there were clinics. Most of them were run by the government, but those in charge expected bribes in return for treatment, often making it too expensive for people from rural areas.

Emily found herself thinking about the skin conditions she'd seen and felt certain she could do something about them with the simple steroid creams available in any drug store stateside. She was especially concerned about the children and was thinking out loud when she looked questioningly at Long and asked, "If I give you some money and a list of supplies, could you find a way to get them here?"

Long hadn't been expecting this and hesitated before answering. "I'm sure we'd find a way, but the villagers wouldn't know what to do with them. They'd need someone with experience or, at least, someone to show them what to do."

"I'm working on that," Emily replied as she turned this over in her mind. She might be able to do something about the minor conditions she'd seen, but almost any help was too late for those suffering from injuries sustained during the war. And there was nothing she could do about the psychological scars. The war generation must still carry wounds that could not be seen, wounds that could not heal. She recalled their meeting with Long's mother in the park and wondered if her apparent acceptance of the hand life had dealt her was the result of time, religion – or something in the psyche of the Vietnamese people. They had had to overcome so much just to survive.

When one of the local women, whose leg ended in a stump, offered them rice balls for breakfast, they gratefully accepted and washed them down with hot tea. Long knew the Americans were not accustomed to this sort of breakfast. What was it that Americans ate? Pancakes? He remembered pancakes from a movie.

"Can you ask her what happened to her leg?" Emily turned to Long again for help. The woman replied that she had lost it when a landmine exploded twenty years ago. It was just as Emily thought. The woman had managed life on a stump all these years. If she'd been lucky enough to be born where there was medical help, she might at least have had a prosthetic lower leg and foot. She might well blame the Americans for her injuries, but she was still able to share her food with them. It was humbling.

As they drank their tea, sitting on mats near one of the huts, villagers came by to stare and to chat. Tom's few words of Vietnamese and a lot of sign language stretched the limits of communication, which often resulted in inexplicable giggles from their hosts. Tom and Emily were beginning to think they probably ought to get moving when they noticed what seemed to be an animated conversation between Long and a wiry little man with wispy gray hair, holding a staff that was taller than he was.

"Who's your friend?" Emily asked.

"This is Ho and he's agreed to be your new guide," Long replied with a look of satisfaction.

"Oh," Emily said, clearly disappointed.

"Is this a problem?"

"Well, no, but I thought you'd be coming with us."

"Oh, I am. You still need a translator, but we need local help. Ho comes highly recommended. They all say he knows every centimeter of this province and can safely guide us anywhere we want to go. Besides, he's fascinated by you Americans, and he's eager to come along."

Tom looked Ho up and down. He looked old even to Tom. "Are you sure he's going to make it? We have a lot of jungle and quite a climb ahead of us," Tom asked doubtfully.

"These villagers are made of tough stuff; I get the feeling Ho here will outlive us all."

"Alright then, I guess we can add another soldier to our own Echo company," Tom said with a little smile and a hint of irony.

Even though he couldn't understand a word, Ho had been watching the exchanges and broke into a huge gap-toothed grin. Long's translation resulted in enthusiastic gestures and a lot of pointing toward the tree line. The more he talked, the more Long's face reflected a serious conversation.

"What's he saying?" asked Emily.

"Every year in Vietnam, about 1,500 people die from landmines and bombs from the war. About 20 percent of the countryside has yet to be cleared. Apparently, a lot of work has been done in this area, but there are no guarantees there won't be hazards where we are going."

Emily looked horrified.

"I read somewhere that more bombs were dropped on Vietnam than all the bombs dropped by the Allies in World War II," Tom commented, "not to mention that both sides were laying traps. Do we have to worry about punji pits?" Tom asked, directing his question to Long.

There was a brief discourse with Ho. "No, those sorts of things will have decomposed or been eaten away by insects. Ho thinks we'll be fine, but watch where you're walking and, if you see anything metallic, move away from it."

Tom remembered the hillside littered with all kinds of traps and mines. If there was anything in the area, that was the likely spot – and it was exactly where they were heading. He looked at Emily, "I hadn't stopped to think there might be a present-day danger. I think you ought to stay behind in the village. This is my journey and I have no right to put you in harm's way. I would never forgive myself if anything happened to you."

Emily considered this. She hadn't realized the possible danger, either; maybe she *should* stay behind. It was a lot to take in, but she was seeing a Vietnam that she would never have seen had she been on her own. Well, she had hoped for an adventure, and the element of danger would certainly add to the experience. This was a chance to prove that she was a woman who could face up to adversity and come out the other side. Besides, it would make a great Instagram post.

Long interrupted her thoughts to agree with Tom, saying, "It's not my business, but I think your grandfather is right. There's no need for you to go."

"Yes, yes there is," Emily said decisively, her mind made up. "Maybe this is Grandpa's journey, but I'm on it, too. I didn't exactly get a vote, but I've come this far, and I'm here now. I'm going the whole way," she said, glaring at the three men in front of her, defying them to argue.

Long and Tom looked at each other and silently acquiesced. "I guess you're old enough to make your own decisions," said Tom, "but there's one condition: Ho may be the guide, but I'm the lead man and you – all of you – will obey my orders, without question. I don't want to lose anyone on this trek, so it's safety first. Got that?" Both Emily and Long saw the grit in Tom's eyes and heard the determination in his voice. They nodded their agreement.

Ho looked confused and spoke to Long while pointing at Emily. He had picked up on the question of whether she would go with them. Emily had no idea what the two men said, but Ho looked her over, nodded and laughed. She had no idea why.

***

It didn't take long for the dirt track of the village to become an overgrown mess of vegetation, but the jungle canopy offered welcome protection from the burning rays of the tropical sun. Strange noises echoed through the foliage, but Emily didn't know if they came from birds or animals. She was in as alien an environment as a girl from the Chicago suburbs could imagine.

This was not a Disney family-friendly jungle but a real primeval rainforest. It was one of the things she had wanted to experience on her trip, but now that she was here, her mind kept slipping back to the time of the war. She blamed her grandfather for that. But the short stay in the village had provided time to reflect on what those brutal years had meant for the Vietnamese people. She had done some Google searches before leaving home and had found that casualty statistics for the Vietnamese, including both military and civilians, varied widely but were thought to be well over a million. A million! She couldn't get her head around it. A million dead Vietnamese – and the Americans had lost! Can you really lose a war when the other side takes a million casualties?

The Americans had been the aggressors, that much was certain, but were those young G.I.s victims too? Her research had also revealed that nearly three million Americans had served in Vietnam during the course of the war; more than 300,000 were injured and nearly 60,000 had died. Casualty figures never made for pleasant reading but these exposed a shocking disparity between the two sides. There had been draft dodgers, of course, but of those who had volunteered or were drafted, how many would have chosen to gamble their futures, their very lives on the decisions made by politically motivated leaders if they had known the extent of their ignorance? Even early on it was said that the war was unwinnable, so why did it take long years of death and destruction – on both sides – to bow to the inevitable?

Things were far from black and white Emily thought as she jumped when a colorful bird squawked overhead and then looked down to see something black on her wrist. She held her arm up and recoiled in horror when she saw a gelatinous black worm, a leech. With the rational part of her mind, she knew that she had a lighter for just such an event; the correct procedure was to burn the leech at the loose end and it would fall off. But the other part of her mind was so revolted by it that she couldn't use her rational mind. The instructions in the manual were all well and good, but a blood-sucking leech, fat on *her* blood, was now dangling from her wrist. She shrieked and slapped at the parasite, which flew off into a nearby bush.

She looked down and saw that the wound had already scabbed with a black crust. She walked on for a minute but knew what she felt wasn't quite right. She looked down again and realized that it was not a scab she saw, but the head of the leech still embedded in her arm. This time she didn't yell but sighed, saying, "You win, Mother Nature," and peeled it off.

Now came the blood. The leech's head had acted as a plug and its teeth had done an excellent job of cutting through her skin. Having heard Emily's screech, both Long and her grandfather were now at her side. After a quick inspection, they staunched the flow of blood, treated the wound with disinfectant and gave her a band-aid. They were very matter-of-fact about it all, so she calmly thanked them and, drama over, continued along the dense undergrowth.

Determined now to prove her bravery credentials, Emily quickly rebounded and was ready to take some shots and a couple of selfies to preserve for the future the fact that she had really done all of this. As she framed an exotic flower, she caught sight of her grandfather following Ho who used his staff and a very big knife to clear the path ahead. Ah yes, she sighed, her grandfather had taken over her travel plans, but she was opening up to new ways of thinking about his time here. She was beginning to understand his urge to come back when it dawned on her that this environment was difficult enough under the best of circumstances. What would it be like fighting a war? She jogged to catch up and asked, "Grandpa, how did you manage to fight in these conditions?"

Tom was breathing heavily and took the opportunity to pause his efforts. He removed his Cubs' cap and pulled out his handkerchief to wipe his brow, saying, "With great difficulty, and now you can see the problem with the whole American strategy."

Long realized exactly what Tom meant. Even though Vietnam had urban areas, with millions of city dwellers, the war was largely fought in the jungles, and they were currently making their way through perfect ambush country. Any sizeable force walking through an area like this would be easy to spot. At the same time, the enemy could easily creep past them or lie in wait. Long thought of his father. He didn't know exactly where he had fought, but he could all too easily imagine him crouched by a tree trunk, scanning the few feet in front of him for movement. He was pretty sure this jungle, and many more just like it, could engulf an entire army, and no one would come out. In a way that's what happened to the Americans.

"We tried to get rid of the dense foliage with something called Agent Orange. It was like weed killer for jungles."

"I think I've heard about Agent Orange ... "

"Sounds like a good idea except pumping thousands of tons of chemicals into the air didn't turn out to be all that great for animals or humans, " Tom continued.

"I remember two children in my class at school were born with defects from the defoliant," Long said quietly.

Emily was appalled, but all she could muster was, "I didn't know." It sounded pathetic; it was pathetic, but she was still trying to take in what the men were saying. Was the military always so intent on winning that it completely disregarded the civilian cost?

Meanwhile, Ho had turned back to see what was causing the delay, muttering and shaking his head as he approached the hopeless trio. It was clear that he wanted to keep moving. Tom pocketed his handkerchief and checked that the lighter was still there before setting off again. Long followed behind him, and Emily trailed Long. She was mulling over the implications of what she had just heard and forgot to look where she was going - until she felt something hard and metallic push down under her foot. She froze. "Grandpa ..." Emily called out weakly.

Tom knew instantly that something was wrong and he spun around to see his granddaughter frozen to the spot, a look of terror on her face.

"What is it?" he asked, rushing back.

"I have just stepped on something metal and felt it push down."

Tom felt his heart sink and his stomach churn. He and Long exchanged looks, which meant that they both understood the situation. Ho had warned them of possible dangers, but Tom had been thinking about the area around the hill. Could the mines the VC had laid for him decades ago now claim the life of his granddaughter? He would not allow it.

Ho sized up the situation and called out something in Vietnamese.

"Wait!" called out Long.

"What is it?" Tom said tetchily.

"Ho says that usually if you find one mine, there are likely to be others nearby."

"I'll take that chance," Tom said as he continued toward Emily, keeping his eyes on the ground. When he was standing in front of her, he could see she was shaking with fear, and that was a problem. If her foot started trembled, it could trigger the mine.

"Now, honey, I know you are scared, but I need you to take a deep breath and stay calm."

"I *am* fucking calm," snapped Emily as tears filled her eyes.

Tom looked around. He would have killed for a k-bar, but the only useful knife available was Ho's. Tom looked up and signaled that he was coming for the machete and Ho met him halfway. Tom needed to use the blade to slide in and hold down the pressure plate while Emily stepped off safely. Well, that was the plan, the only one available, and it had to work. What he'd do after that was too far in the future.

Tom dug deep into his memories about MD-82s and M14 anti-personnel landmines, trying to recall anything useful, when, out of the corner of his eye, he saw Long moving in to help. Tom raised the palm of his hand. "Don't move," he ordered. "I don't want to turn one life-threatening situation into two. At least I've had some experience of this." Fifty-year-old experience he thought, but right now, this old man was the best hope his granddaughter had for getting out of this alive. He laid the machete on the ground, moved closer to Emily and looked into eyes filled with panic and fear.

"It's okay, honey, I'm going fix this," he spoke softly, just as he had done so many times when Emily was little. She slowly nodded her understanding and became a statue even though every fiber of her body was screaming at her to run.

"I need you to stand absolutely still because I'm going to have a look at whatever it is you're standing on."

Emily nodded again, and Tom went down on his hands and knees. He got up close to her foot and saw that there was definitely something metallic underneath it. He knew that the pressure plate was on the top, so he felt around the object and began to dig carefully, using a stick and his fingers. He recognized the thick, clay-like mud on his hands. All too often he had been covered in the stuff. The familiar smell of rotting vegetation clogged his nostrils as he gently prodded rainforest compost.

"Do you know what it is?" Emily whispered.

"No," Tom said flatly as he felt around the cylindrical device. It seemed smaller than he remembered. Corrosion on the sides had tainted the metallic finish, but the browny gold edging was still there. He smiled gently and pushed his stick into the side of the object.

Emily felt the movement. "Careful!" she implored.

The metal crumbled under the pressure and revealed mud inside. Tom had recognized the finish. It was not a mine; it was an empty, upside-down C-ration container.

Tom chuckled to himself as relief washed over him. The situation had gone from deadly serious to farcical in a matter of seconds, and he laughed as he said, "It's okay. You can move now."

Emily couldn't quite believe her ears. "What's so funny?"

"Sorry, sweetie, sorry. Everything's fine; it's just an empty C-ration can."

"A what?"

"It's a can that used to have food in it. Some G.I. didn't take it with him and, fifty years later, you stepped on his trash."

Emily moved her foot and saw what looked like a rusty tuna can half-buried in the dirt. She let out a sob and flung herself into her grandfather's arms, both of them in tears. Ho and Long understood that the threat had passed and laughed when Tom prized the can out of the ground to show them.

The danger may have been non-existent, but it made them all more cautious as they pressed on toward the hill. Tom warned them that what had just happened with Emily should be regarded as a dress rehearsal for the hill. He hoped the clearance efforts had been thorough, but they must remain vigilant. Emily didn't need to be persuaded.

Ho was out in front, eagle-eyed and quick; it turned out Long had been right about the surprisingly spry elder. As they approached the foot of the hill, Tom began to recount his role in the battle. He described the machine gun emplacements sweeping the hillside with deadly fire, the cries of the men and the fear of booby traps. Long translated for Ho who told them that the villagers could hear the battle and were terrified for their lives. To them, it sounded like dragons clashing in a storm.

Emily looked at the steep incline and tried to imagine charging up the hill while under enemy machine gun fire. It must have been carnage. Ho was already halfway up while Tom guided Emily and Long and looked everywhere for the opening to the tunnel that Mo and Alabama had entered all those years ago. Time had erased it.

Tom's old legs found new vigor as they approached the ridgeline and went over the top. Although the jungle had reclaimed almost everything, the hill was still flat. Thick vegetation squatted on what had been an undistinguished kill zone, but Tom knew where key features had been and poked around with a stick to find any of the slit trenches. When he saw a furrow running across the center, he knew he'd found the main trench line. Now shallow and covered with lush foliage, it was still the hill's most obvious feature.

Emily had been caught up in Tom's story of the battle and realized that this flat-topped hill would be the perfect place to shoot at anyone dumb enough to come over the ridge. When Tom began to recount the napalm drop, both Emily and Long knew they were standing on the site of what had been a man-made inferno. As the trees rustled in the breeze, Emily imagined the sound of burning and, despite the heat, felt a shiver run down her spine.

Subdued by the knowledge of events that had taken place here, the three of them stood surveying a spectacular view. Experiencing it now in peacetime, Tom realized a lot had passed him by. War had made the countryside ugly; peace allowed it to be beautiful once again. He was seeing everything with new eyes and was struck now by Vietnam's splendor. The whole scene might have been poetic had Ho not been standing off to the side relieving himself over the edge.

It had been a tough morning. They were physically and emotionally exhausted. No one argued when Ho indicated it was time to rest and produced food the villagers had so generously provided. Ready to put the horrors of war behind them, they found a patch of shade and sat down to eat. The local food restored them and their spirits began to rise again.

"What's next?" Emily asked, assuming they'd be turning back.

Tom pointed to the ridge of hills to the north. "That," he said.

Emily looked up at the forbidding terrain. Surely he could not be serious.

***

Jessica refreshed the page again. Where was Emily? When she had last heard from her, she was heading off to a village in the Vietnamese countryside. She couldn't wait to see the pictures, but Emily had gone dark for more than twenty-four hours, and that was almost the same as being dead. Jessica was worried about this big change in routine. She didn't want to call Em's mom but felt she had no option.

Sarah was sitting down to dinner with her husband David, her son John and the girlfriend Debbie, who seemed to be a going concern. They were all tucking into a hearty meatloaf with mashed potatoes and gravy when someone's phone rang.

"Now, John, what did we say about phones at the table?" his mother said sternly.

John smiled slyly. "You're right, Mom, but that's not my phone."

Sarah stared at Debbie, who was now looking down at her plate of food. She knew the phone wasn't hers, but she still felt guilty. Sarah was about to bring her husband into the line of fire when she realized the sound was coming from behind her. It was her phone. It rang so rarely, she didn't recognize the ringtone. "Excuse me," she said, looking mildly embarrassed as she got up.

"But I thought the rule was 'no phone calls at the table'," John said, enjoying the moral high ground.

"Don't," Sarah said, giving him a withering look. "Hello?" she said, not recognizing the number that flashed up on the screen.

"Hi, Mrs. Hawkins. This is Jessica."

"Oh, hi," Sarah said. "Is everything alright?"

"Look, I don't want to alarm you, but Emily and I talk pretty regularly online, and I haven't heard from her for over twenty-four hours. So I'm just wondering if you know anything," explained Jessica in what she hoped was her casual voice.

"Oh, you girls do like to talk, don't you?" Sarah said, somewhat condescendingly.

"Yes, yes we do," Jessica said politely, not mistaking the tone but letting it pass for the sake of information.

"Everything's okay; I spoke to her yesterday. She was planning to go with her grandfather to a village a couple of hours from the city."

"Oh, I knew that, but I haven't heard from her since."

"Well, from what I understand, the village is well off the beaten path. Emily thought they'd have wi-fi, but I'm not so sure. Even if they do, it's probably unreliable."

"Surely it's not that backward, is it?"

"It's probably like rural areas here where reception is sometimes difficult, but she'll be back online once they return to the city. I think she had some concerns about going off into the countryside, but they're taking a guide with them."

Jessica was taken aback. She had assumed she would have the edge on Em's news, but it seems her friend had more recently and more thoroughly filled in her mother. It probably had to do with the fact that she was traveling with Sarah's father. Jessica knew Em had been toying with the idea of striking out on her own, so did this mean things had taken a turn for the better?

"Gosh, it sounds like she's having a real adventure, but it's good to know they have a guide. I hope things are going well."

"I don't think there's any reason to worry and, frankly, if there were, I'd be the first in line."

Emily's attempts to broaden her horizons were rippling across everyone she knew.

***

A strange mood permeated the soldiers. It had been a tough day: two firefights, one in the morning and then an even bigger one in the afternoon. It had also been a bloody day, with nineteen men dead and twenty-eight wounded. But the enemy had been hit hard. The VC kill count was ninety-six ... that they could find. General Westmoreland would be happy with that kind of ratio. It was good to have a stand-up fight with the usually elusive enemy, but for the men remaining, there were painful gaps in their ranks. While the men of Tom's squad couldn't help but talk about

Alabama, Mo was quiet that night, sitting apart from the group, absorbed in his thoughts.

But to the victors, the spoils. Humby's squad had returned to the village and brought the butchered water buffalo back to the encampment. Now the smell of barbequed beef filled everyone's nostrils, making bellies rumble and mouths salivate. There was food aplenty and music blaring out from the radio. It could almost have been a cookout back home. The only thing missing – well, almost the only thing missing - was cold beer. The men had returned from a successful hunt. Only their helmets and uniforms revealed them to be a particular kind of hunter.

Most of the squad were having fun, letting off steam but, like Mo, Tom was sitting off to the side. He chewed absent-mindedly on his buffalo steak as he stared into the fire. He had lost a squadmate and killed a baby, all in one day. The realization was overwhelming. Eddie sat down beside him. "What's up, man?" he asked, giving Tom the time he needed to reply.

"You know how those demonstrators back home call us 'baby killers'?"

Eddie knew where this was going. "Yeah, brother."

"I always thought that was just lefty hysteria. Turns out they're right, and I am one of them."

"Okay, but let's say you somehow knew there was a crib behind that wall, so you chose to push through the door. You and probably half the squad would have died doing that, and the kid would still have died in the crossfire."

"I dunno," Tom said softly.

"Well, I do. This whole war is one big, steaming pile of bullshit, and today was the biggest pile of bullshit to be added to the whole stinking mess. Now you and I and everyone around us did not make this pile of bullshit. Bullshit comes from bulls, and we ain't bulls. No, we are just the poor bastards who have to stand on this gigantic pile of steaming bullshit, shoveling it around to stop the whole shit pile from toppling over."

Tom managed a weak laugh. "That's a subtle metaphor you've got going there, Eddie, my man."

"Why, thank you. I'm planning on going to Harvard to study poetry if I make it back." He chuckled to himself as Skoberne approached, his eyes on Tom. "Private First Class Moretti, with me."

Skoberne wanted a quiet word with Tom away from the squad. He knew Tom was mentally stuck in the events of the day, scrabbling around trying to pick up the shards of his shattered spirit. Skoberne had a pretty good idea of how Tom felt. He had taken the baby from her cot and it had devastated him too. "You've had a hard day, and I know there's nothing I can say that can change what happened. I also know you won't believe me when I tell you that you did the right thing." Skoberne paused before continuing, "Ordinarily I would be putting you in for a citation. Your quick thinking saved lives today, but under the circumstances, I'm guessing you wouldn't want it."

Tears welled up in Tom's eyes. "I killed a baby, sir."

"I know."

"I don't think I'll ever get over it," Tom replied as he sniffed, fighting back tears.

"I understand that, Moretti. War makes monsters of us all and I don't have any easy answers. What I do know is that Echo company took the fight to the enemy and won, but sometimes life punishes us even when we do the right thing."

"I'm finding that out, sir."

"I'm not going to try and assuage the guilt I know you feel, but if you ever want to talk about things, you can always come to me."

"Thank you, sir," Tom replied as Ortiz came running up. He paused as he recognized the two men were deep in conversation and coughed politely before telling Skoberne the captain wanted to see him. The lieutenant put a hand on Tom's shoulder before heading off to the VC bunker that Captain de Bruin had turned into his field HQ.

De Bruin stood behind a roughly constructed wooden table, chewing on a generous portion of the water buffalo, his attention focused on a map on the table. The makeshift office was illuminated by a single VC paraffin lamp. He looked up when Skoberne and the other lieutenants walked in together. "Gentlemen, it's been an intense but productive day."

Skoberne wasn't sure he would describe the day in quite the same way, but he knew what the captain meant.

"We've taken the fight to the enemy and crushed them. However, I am under no illusions. We lost good men and the fighting was hard, but that's why I've allowed the men to break protocol and have a cookout. They need to taste victory." De Bruin ate another mouthful. "And today victory tastes a lot like steak," he said with a smile.

The men chuckled.

"But now we must look at the next phase of the operation," de Bruin said, his demeanor becoming more serious. "This hilltop seems to be the enemy's forward base of operations. That ridge of high terrain stretching to the northwest seems to be a center of enemy activity. Intel suggests it's where supplies and men are concentrated and then distributed from a branch of the Ho Chi Minh Trail."

De Bruin pointed to the map, and Skoberne and the others all looked closely. "We are going to take the three companies and push up through these hills to clear out the enemy, right on the border with Cambodia. HQ suggests that this move will draw in more VC as Charlie doesn't want to lose the high ground. We are going to bleed them dry on these slopes."

Skoberne felt obliged to challenge the plan. "But sir, won't they know we're coming?"

"Yes, absolutely. We are hoping they know because this will concentrate their forces. ARVN heavy mortar teams will be brought in tomorrow. We will help them set up here on this hill, and they will act as artillery support. We will have air support from multiple aircraft, the usual ordinance, high explosive napalm as well as the new AC-130s. It's a

Hercules transport where they've mounted 4 × 7.62 mm miniguns and 4 × 20 mm M61 Vulcan cannons to the side. The damn thing can fire 40,000 rounds in a minute. That's not air support, that's a hailstorm of metal. The plan is victory through annihilation."

The officers looked at each other apprehensively. The plan sounded like they had an almost indecent amount of support, but they'd all looked into the distance and seen those high ridges. DeBruin might call them hills, but they looked like mountains to everyone else. This would be a hard trek and the element of surprise was gone.

"Thank you, gentlemen. Get your boys to wrap things up out there and get some shut-eye. We are up tomorrow at zero-five-thirty to help set up the ARVN mortars before we start heading into the hills."

***

A strange mood permeated Emily as the four of them hiked on through the jungle. On the one hand, she had to acknowledge that this exposure to the Vietnamese interior was exactly what she had hoped for, with or without her grandfather. But at the same time, her head was spinning with the revelations. He hadn't been joking when he'd warned that his war stories would be hard to hear, but she was beginning to understand that these young Americans had been put in impossible situations. No sane person would choose to infiltrate an enemy tunnel, but neither would he choose to be shot at. No sane person would choose to harm a baby, but neither would he choose to put squadmates in the firing line. No sane person would choose to come across the globe to fight … for what? Was communism that dangerous? What was the threat to America? What the hell had her grandfather – or any of them – given up their young lives for? Certainly nothing that seemed to make any sense to her. Maybe not to them, either.

What a strange little band they were Emily thought, all coming at the war from different perspectives, each one reliving the war in their own way. Her grandfather had ghosts to lay to rest. She had not wanted any part of this, but having allowed herself to be pulled into the complexities of the past, found that now she, too, wanted a sense of resolution. And then there was Long, whose calming presence made him a kind of peacemaker. What was all this to him? And Ho? Because of his small frame and jolly demeanor, she couldn't help but think of him as a tropical version of one of Santa's elves. She couldn't make him out but had a sneaky suspicion he was along for the entertainment almost as much as the money. She was pretty sure he had little regard for Americans.

Long had no idea what was going to happen next. A simple trip to the countryside was taking a new turn every day and, while he was glad to be along for the ride, he still had some concerns. The Americans seemed to assume that all Vietnamese were at home in the jungle. The reality was that, whichever side they were on in the war, the Vietnamese had been learning to adapt to the jungle environment at the same time as the foreigners. Long had been brought up with the national story of brave men fighting the evil colonial powers, and now, here he was, literally on the warpath.

Tom was feeling every year of his age and every pound of his weight and couldn't help the odd grunt that accompanied the ever-demanding effort to keep up with Ho. No one knew how old he was, not even Ho, but it was clear that the man had almost supernatural stamina that put the others to shame. No doubt his lean build was an advantage in this rugged terrain. As they carefully picked their way through the undergrowth, a line of red ants or the tail of a snake slithering away served as reminders that there were dangers in the jungle that weren't man-made.

"Wouldn't it be cool if we saw a tiger," Emily said, wiping the sweat from her face.

"Yes, I would love to see one, but Ho told me there aren't any left in this region," Long replied, stretching his back to get some relief from his pack.

"What a shame. Tigers are one of the most beautiful creatures in the world and to see them in their natural habitat would be a rare privilege."

"A privilege, yes, but as Ho pointed out, it would also be the last thing we would see. To a tiger, we would be lunch."

When they came to a stream, they found a relatively clear, level spot where they could spend the night. Everyone was exhausted as much from the heat as from their physical exertions. While the others went to get water, Tom laid out their camp with military precision. His instinct was to do everything as quietly as possible so as not to alert the enemy, but of course, there was no enemy, there was no war – just the reflexive thinking that his surroundings brought to the fore. They had had all day to get used to the sounds of the jungle, but Tom had never become accustomed to them, not now, not back then. They always made him think of primeval beasts. The jungle was currently being benevolent, but he knew that could change in a heartbeat.

As the light faded, they gathered around the campfire and ate a simple meal. The jungle canopy obscured any light from the heavens, and the darkness seemed somehow magnified. Emily had not previously realized the enormous comfort of a fire.

"Tell me about your wife," Long said, turning to Tom.

Emily glanced at her grandfather to see what he made of this. It would never have occurred to her to say anything so bold on a subject she herself found painful. She was glad to be off the topic of the war, but this reminder that she had lost her lovely grandmother pierced her heart anew.

"I was always surprised she married me," Tom said, staring into the fire. After reliving the traumas of the war, this was a chance to embrace the best part of his past. "She had the pick of the guys, and I had to leave to fight in the war, but she waited for me. I couldn't believe my luck. And she was one of the few people who could see both sides of the debate. When I came home, I had some people slap me on the back and call me an all-American hero; others spat at me and called me a baby killer. The first were trying to show support, but they were misguided, and the anger from the others was justified. Elaine could see both points of view, but she was always an oasis of calm – and smart enough to understand what I needed. It took time for me – for most of us – to fully come home. But she was there, waiting and patient, and she did everything she could to put me back together. She wanted me … not the soldier … just me."

For Emily, this was a new way of looking at the gray-haired woman who baked delicious cookies and indulged her every whim. She'd never thought about her grandmother as a young woman who had fallen for her grandfather, that they had a love story of their own. To Emily, she'd been the kind and cuddly person who would always be there, always ready to make things right for her. What she missed about that relationship she would never find in anyone else, and she realized that the same thing was true for her grandfather. People can't be replaced.

"She told me she had found her man and nothing was going to put her off. I don't know what she saw in me. Do men ever? I've always had this sneaking suspicion that women marry beneath them. Maybe that explains why they're always trying to fix us," he said with a little chuckle. "I guess most of us do need fixin'."

Long thought about his own wife. She had certainly married beneath her, and she was always trying to fix him, he thought, smiling to himself. She could have done so much better, but she had stuck by him.

"Anyway, we got married, started a family. I joined the fire department, and she always fretted that I would die in some house fire, but here I am," Tom sighed and paused before continuing. "She loved music and she was talented. She could have had a career as a classical pianist."

A memory flashed up in Emily's head. She had forgotten. As a little girl, she would sit on her grandmother's lap and place her little hands on her grandmother's as she played the piano. Emily was fascinated by the beautiful melodies she heard as their fingers moved together over the black and white keys. It was magic.

"When she wasn't working or cooking or raising kids, she would play the piano. That's the thing about life; it has a habit of getting in the way of what you planned to do. I guess that's why I'm here now. I don't have a job anymore. My children are all grown up and have their own lives, and now, my best friend, my life companion is gone. I no longer have any excuse for not doing what I've needed to do and revisit the past." Tom lowered his head and said softly, "I feel like she's here with me in Vietnam. It's funny because she never had anything to do with the place except to help me pick up the pieces when I got back. Maybe she wants to see me through to the end of the journey."

Ho had rejected the offer to share a tent with Long and was snoring peacefully on his mat not far away, signaling that it was time they all turned in. After the abundant spraying of insect repellant, the trio settled down to fitful sleep. Even without the stirring of memories, Tom had never had a good night's sleep in the jungle. It was nature's revenge for daring to enter her realm.

When they surfaced the next morning, Ho was ready with some tea, chattering to them, obviously urging them on. He was ready to go and didn't see why they shouldn't be, too. They quickly ate some breakfast and headed off toward the slope.

Tom looked up ahead at a trail of ever-increasing rises and was filled with a sense of trepidation. He was closing in on the site of their defeat five decades ago, but it was more than that. The defeat had been a military one, but his failure to keep a promise was personal. The skies were darkening and the heavy clouds overhead warned of a coming storm. The weather matched his mood and the turmoil inside him. The dead baby, the napalm firestorm, the men who died, the shame, the guilt, the fear were all coming together on this mountain. The enemy, then and now, was here.

"We're close," Tom whispered.

***

The next morning Lieutenant Skoberne ordered the platoon to help set up the M30 heavy mortars for the ARVN troops. The South Vietnamese soldiers had the nearly 700-pound mortars disassembled into their component parts and split up amongst them. They were going to use the recently conquered flat-topped hill as a firebase to launch their shells into enemy positions in the hills ahead of them. It was a solid if uninspired plan.

Supply trucks had pulled into the village in the valley below, and it was the job of Tom's platoon to hump the shells up to where the mortars were being set up. Each shell weighed twenty-seven pounds, so the soldiers could manage only two at a time. This was going to be intense, sweaty work. All the men were stripped down to their t-shirts or went bare-chested, their helmets and rifles the only sign that they were soldiers and not a bunch of Boy Scouts on some kind of bizarre camping trip.

Traveling down to the village was easy and gave the men a chance to refill canteens with cold water from the stream. The purification tablets added that unmistakable chemical tang, but the water's cool temperature compensated for that. The fact that it was in plentiful supply meant not only that it slaked thirsts, but that it could be poured over their heads to bring the temperature down.

But it was the slog back up the hill that produced its own special hell. The bombs had to be carried gingerly; the amount of high explosive and white phosphorous in them would annihilate a clumsy soldier in the blink of an eye. The men took care with their footing, but the weight of the shells quickly sapped their youthful energy.

Eddie had positioned himself and his machine gun on a slope above them. He couldn't carry it and mortar shells, and it was more important that he use this perfect defensive weapon to protect the base.

Ortiz had the radio on his back so that he could communicate instantly if they needed to fight off an ambush. He saw Mo curse under his breath when he briefly lost his footing and stumbled. "Hey, now you know how I feel every day," he shouted.

"Say what?" Mo fired back testily.

"This radio, it's a damn sight heavier than your shotgun and mortar rounds, and I still have to carry my rifle. Right now, you guys are living my life."

"Can it, you two," Skoberne said, sensing trouble between the two soldiers. It was never a good thing when both men were armed, and one of them was lugging over fifty pounds of high explosives.

The first time going up the hill, Tom had walked with ARVN troops carrying their disassembled mortars. Even as they carried their loads, they were smiling and chatting with each other. The next time Tom reached the top, the South Vietnamese troops had reassembled their mortars and were beginning to dig them in. By his third trip, they had completed set up and were now standing around, socializing and smoking.

Tom was more than annoyed. Now that they had finished setting up, why couldn't they help carry all the damn munitions? The Americans were carrying their supplies for their mortars after all. Tom noticed others making the same observation and commenting, but Zielinski and the other sergeants ordered silence on the subject. Every time Tom had been around ARVN troops, they seemed to be having a good time and goofing off. Why did the North get all the Vietnamese with fire in their bellies and an innate desire to fight whereas the South seemed to have troops who treated the whole war as some kind of camping holiday?

After a day of back-breaking work, the platoon settled in for another night's sleep on the hill. While the rest of the three companies had pushed forward, their platoon had made zero progress, but at least the mortar teams were now well set up, with enough ammunition to call down fire support for a week.

"Drop your cocks, and grab your socks," came the call from Zielinski as he roamed around the sleeping men to get them up. Tom rubbed his eyes. It was dawn. He looked blearily at the sight of Eddie yawning and reaching for the day's first cigarette.

"You know those will kill you," Tom said. It was part of a daily routine that the both of them had begun to feel was a good luck ritual.

"Hey, man, if I get to die of lung cancer, I'll be one lucky sonofabitch."

Both of them smiled and proceeded to gear up for whatever was ahead of them. They climbed all day and ran into numerous natural obstacles, from waterfalls to sinkholes. The heat was oppressive, and Tom found himself picking leeches off his skin several times that morning. The men were still tired after hauling mortar rounds the previous day, and now they were carrying extra ammo for the battle ahead of them. Tom spied one desperate soldier getting rid of belts of M60 ammunition by throwing them into a forest pool, just to lighten his load and get some relief on that hot and humid day. Tom caught his eye and glared at him. The soldier just shrugged in response.

They took turns at point, but there was little opportunity for anyone to act as flankers because the way up had steep drop-offs on either side. There was no denying that the terrain was becoming more mountainous, and the trail was becoming narrower. The brutal climb took them above the tree line where the views were spectacular, but the beauty of the mountains was lost on men who were focused on putting one foot ahead of the other as they made their way to certain battle.

Just before noon, after a wearying morning, they heard the sound of gunfire in the distance. Moments later, Ortiz's radio crackled awake. The vanguard of the force had just made contact with the VC base. Ortiz listened intently; his ability to hear the battle from multiple viewpoints gave him a secret thrill of omnipotence. Then he heard the request for mortar support. Moments later, the deep-throated whooshing noise of the mortars hurling their projectiles in a lazy arc could be heard from below. The platoon cheered. It was good to know their hard work was paying off. A few seconds later and the deep-bass sound of 4.2-inch mortar rounds detonating on the front lines of the enemy raised a new roar of approval.

"Eat high explosives, Charlie!" Tom shouted.

The sound reinvigorated the men to press on. The other companies needed their help, and true to Skoberne's word, they had the right amount of support for a change. The mortars fired non-stop, producing a cacophony that boosted morale. But as the barrage persisted, some of the men began to look at each other questioningly. Surely the mortars could stop now. But on and on they fired. "Are those fuckers going to keep on firing 'til they use up all that ammo we lugged up that hill?" Mo complained.

The echoes of explosive mortar rounds came back in reply. The men pushed on under their incessant roar, the smiles wiped from their faces. Yes, it appeared that once they started to fire, the ARVN mortar team was going to keep firing until they didn't have anything left; presumably, they could then go home or, at least, leave the war zone. Tom's face hardened as he watched all that back-breaking work disappear, literally, in a puff of smoke.

Eventually, after what felt like an eternity of firing, the mortars went quiet. "I guess they finally ran out," Tom observed dryly.

"Or their tubes got too hot," Ortiz replied.

"I'd like to heat up their fucking tubes," muttered Zielinski.

Even though it was just the tiniest moment of insubordination from the sergeant, it was enough to shut everyone up. Zielinski did not break ranks and any doubts he had he always kept to himself. He knew that was the way things went in the army, but right now, after seeing his men break their backs to support ARVN troops, he was disgusted by their reckless, cowboy attitude and their lack of respect for the work of those supporting them. Why was he putting himself and other Americans in harm's way to defend their country when they couldn't follow basic orders? He knew his comment would shock, but it had slipped out before he'd realized he was speaking out loud. After that, he remained silent unless it was to issue orders.

The platoon continued to scramble their way up the ridge toward the sound of gunfire. The radio was telling the story after the mortars fell silent. The VC had lost a few men in the initial bombardment, but after that, they had kept their heads down. The shelling had allowed the Americans to reposition, but once the smoke cleared, the two sides were fighting each other at almost point-blank range.

The enemy was entrenched, motivated and determined to fight for every inch, and Tom was heading straight for them.

***

The storm came on quickly and the trail offered no place for respite as Tom, Ho, Emily and Long headed up the narrow path. When the heavens erupted, the rains poured down in an instant deluge as if a giant faucet in the sky had been turned on. It was a noisy rain as pounding water hit hard stone and lashed the jungle's luxuriant foliage. The force of the water dug up small stones and splashed jungle mud. It washed around a gigantic boulder sitting at right angles to the side of the track and threatened to engulf the absorbent moss around its base.

Tom felt the heavy drops smack the peak of his cap, but he had come prepared; he had slogged through too many monsoon rains to get caught out this time and had packed ponchos. There hadn't been a huge selection, so the motley trio were currently enrobed in peach colored waterproofs with two star-crossed lovers gazing into each other's eyes, the message 'Eternal Love' emblazoned in English and Vietnamese across their backs.

Tom had offered one to Ho, who declined, indicating his *nón lá* coolie hat was sufficient protection. Apparently oblivious to the downpour, he watched bemused as the others threw on what he considered to be a foolish item of clothing, then he guffawed and shook his head. Tom considered: they did look like walking candy wrappers.

"Do you know this program? My wife loves it," Long commented.

"Er, no, I just got what was available," shrugged Tom, not realizing the message referred to a TV soap opera.

With nowhere to stop to see out the storm, they continued heading up the steep path, the wind grabbing at the edges of their ponchos. Tom could feel rivulets of sweat pouring down his back as he caught a nose-twitching whiff of his own body. Maybe the ponchos hadn't been such a good idea after all. Either way, they were wet through. Emily must be hating this, he thought to himself.

Emily had given up the fight to stay dry – or clean - as she trudged on, keeping sight of her grandfather just ahead of her. What am I doing in the middle of a tropical storm, on a mountain ridge in Vietnam, she kept asking herself. But she knew the answer. She had wanted to test herself, and this was pushing every boundary she could imagine. It turned out she loved the feel of rain on her face and mud on her legs; it felt animalistic. She wanted to snarl at the sky and lash out at the storm. This was primal and it was thrilling.

Just then a flash of lightning forked across the sky, and the storm roared back at her with the boom of thunder. As exhilarating as it was, it began to dawn on her that the four of them were on their own; nobody knew where they were. As the visibility steadily decreased and the weather worsened, were they in danger?

Ho cried out something as he pointed to the side of the trail.

"What did he say?" Emily shouted to Long.

"Storm's getting worse," Long translated.

"No kidding," Emily said sarcastically, thinking to herself that she didn't need a guide to tell her that.

"He says we'll wait out the storm under that overhang," Long said, indicating a hollow in the hillside. They made their way and ducked through the stream of water that flowed across the overhanging rock. It was an inadequate shelter, but it would have to do.

Long saw the anxious look on Emily's face and nudged Ho for a brief conversation. Ho nodded in agreement. "Monsoon rains arrive suddenly and finish just as quickly," Long explained in an effort to reassure.

"Are we in danger?" Emily asked.

"Why don't you ask your grandfather. I'm just a city boy," Long deflected, not sure of the answer.

"Look, the storm is pretty wild, but it should pass soon enough, in which case we'll be fine," Tom said, hoping he was right.

"And if it doesn't?"

"It will," Tom replied firmly, putting an end to the questions.

They stood silently, side-by-side, looking out, their inner thoughts accompanied by the strident sounds of wind and rain. Ho took the opportunity to fill his canteen from the newly created waterfall in front of them. Emily guessed that he had survived worse things than any threat that might come from unpurified water. Whatever happened, he was sanguine. Did nothing worry this spry old man? As Ho was screwing the cap on, he stepped back to better hear what Long was saying, something that was lost on Emily and Tom.

When Emily started to shiver, Tom leaned over and said, "The rain is leaching your body heat. Although the air temperature is still high, the water is cooling your body. Crouch down so the poncho is touching the ground." Emily obeyed. "Is it okay if I rub your shoulders and back to help you warm up a little?"

The question surprised her. Emily had been grabbed and manhandled by her grandfather on countless occasions; it was his way of showing affection. One of her favorite childhood memories was their game of tag when he would catch her, grab her by the ankles and dangle her upside down. While she giggled uncontrollably, he teased her that he was sweeping the floor with her hair. That was a very long time ago. Now, something fundamental had changed if he felt he needed to ask her permission to give her a backrub.

Emily thought back to the very beginning of this trip and their recent days in the country. Together but separate probably best-summarized things. There had been some harsh words, mainly on her part, not to mention all the words that had remained unsaid. Now he did not want to presume because they had lost their old connection. The painful realization stabbed Emily in the heart and made her gasp. Tom misunderstood and thought she was gasping from the cold, but she nodded consent, and Tom set to work rubbing her back.

The effort Tom was putting in on Emily warmed his own shivering body, and Long, recognizing his own signs of exposure, began to rub his arms and stamp his feet. Ho was clearly unhappy about the stamping and put out a restraining arm when the ground beneath them shifted, and waterlogged earth gave way to a mudslide that threatened to carry Ho to certain death. His eyes widened as his body began to fall. Emily screamed and lunged forward to grab Ho by his left arm, but the momentum was too much for her to counter, and she felt her arms begin to follow him down the side of the cliff. She clung on desperately even as she felt herself being pulled toward the edge. Then everything stopped.

Tom was old; his reactions weren't as quick as Emily's, but she had bought enough time for him to react and grab hold of her around the waist. Now the two of them tried to hold the dangling Ho, who was scrabbling against the mud and stones of the cliffside, trying to find a toehold. His movements threatened to dislodge him from Emily's grasp. "Long, tell Ho to hold still!" she screamed.

Long had frozen in fear as he watched Ho slide away, but he roused himself to shout down to the terrified Ho, who continued his frantic search for a foothold. Emily was now flat out in the mud, desperate to hang onto Ho, while Tom grunted and heaved, trying to make sure Emily didn't go over. By now Long had joined in and had grabbed Tom's waist, adding his strength and weight to the desperate struggle.

"Stay, still!" Long bellowed again in Vietnamese. He didn't want to let go of Tom, but there was some distance between Long and Ho, and with the noise of the storm, he couldn't be sure that Ho could hear him. As lightning flashed across the sky, Ho looked up and saw Emily's desperation. He finally understood and went limp, his body now dangling in thin air.

Emily felt one of her hands losing its grip. She had to let go, taking all of Ho's weight in one hand for the split second it took her second hand to gain a better hold. Thank you, Eric, she thought somewhere in the back of her mind. Ho reached up and clasped onto her slippery, wet arms, one at a time. Tom tried to adjust for the sudden movement, but the four of them slid another couple of inches toward the chasm.

Ho shouted something in Vietnamese. Was it advice? A warning? Tom had no idea. "I can't see what's happening, so what do you want me to do?" Tom shouted, hoping Emily could hear him.

"I've got a grip on Ho, but I can't lift him up, and I'm not sure how much longer I can hang onto him!"

"Okay, you're arms are acting like a rope, a link between you and Ho. The pulling will have to come from me and Long. Your job is to hang onto him any way you can. Long and I are going to start pulling in the opposite direction. We should be able to get gravity working for us. Just keep holding on!"

Tom began to lean back; he could feel his muscles shifting under his skin. Age, it's a sucker's game, he thought. He wished he was younger, stronger, more nimble. If he'd been able to react quicker, his granddaughter wouldn't be in danger now. He had to grit his teeth and find the strength he needed if they had any chance of saving Ho. Tom heaved backward and felt Long working with him.

The storm continued around them; the tension was palpable. As Tom and Long worked together, they felt Emily begin to come toward them, and Ho was, at last, able to find some purchase by walking his feet up the side of the slope. This provided some relief from his dead weight and allowed the others to redouble their efforts and drag him closer to the lip of the cliff edge.

Minutes stretched into an eternity before Ho was scrabbling back over the edge, emerging from below with his familiar gap-toothed grin in place, looking for all the world as if nothing much had happened. But even Ho had felt the strain and collapsed with the others, out of breath, too shattered to do anything other than lay back in the mud.

Everyone was cold, wet and utterly exhausted, and they lay where they were as they slowly began to recover. The rain was subsiding, but darkness had descended, and Emily held a flashlight so Tom could see what he was doing. Even so, conditions were difficult and Tom was feeling tetchy as he fumbled with the tents. He felt a tap on his shoulder and looked around impatiently. Undeterred by the look on Tom's face, Ho launched into what seemed to be some sort of formal speech, the timing of which was a mystery to Tom. He couldn't understand a word Ho was saying and was too tired for games. Then Ho produced a flask and looked earnestly at Tom.

"What's this all about?" Tom asked Long.

"Ho is thanking you. He said that before you came, the only thing he knew about Americans was that they had come to kill and destroy in the past and did senseless and stupid things now. But then you saved his life. He wants to thank you in the only way he knows how. He's offering you some of his own *ruou gao,* rice wine. He's made it himself according to a traditional family recipe. It's his way of saying that because you saved his life, you are now part of his family."

"Oh," Tom said, completely taken aback by this unexpected gesture. He mentally adjusted his mood from irritation to what he hoped came across as graciousness. Rice wine. Tom recalled his previous experience of drinking it that first night in the village. Best go carefully he thought to himself. He took the flask and bowed to acknowledge Ho's gesture; then he looked at Long, not sure of the etiquette. Long nodded and Tom unscrewed the top. He smiled at Ho, took a deep breath and gulped down what he hoped was a sufficiently manly mouthful.

As soon as he'd done it, he knew this particular vintage was not going to go down smoothly. It savaged the tastes buds on his tongue and burned its way down the back of his throat before assaulting his stomach. Tom understood the gesture meant a lot to Ho, so he swallowed the urge to cough and splutter. But he couldn't do anything about his bright red face and grinned insanely through the fire in his belly. He was about to hand the flask back when Ho went straight in for a hug. Between the power of the rice wine and the surprise hug, Tom was reeling, but he had the presence of mind to hug back.

"Congratulations," said Long. "You are now part of Ho's family."

In the gloom, Tom couldn't tell if Long was smirking, but he definitely heard Emily's 'ahhhs' … which reminded him that if anyone deserved a share of Ho's brew, it was Emily. The flask was still in his hand, so he looked at Emily, then nodded to Ho, hoping he understood and agreed with the decision to offer her a drink.

Emily had watched the proceedings and, on behalf of her grandfather, felt quite touched by Ho's gesture. She had seen that her grandfather had done his best to retain his composure through what appeared to be an ordeal by fire, but she had not understood that she, too, would be offered a drink. Now that she had, she knew that to refuse would be more than rude. All eyes were on her as she raised the flask to her mouth. She took just enough to make it appear she had a suitable mouthful and swallowed gingerly, but her cautious approach made no discernible difference to the inferno that roared down the track from her mouth to her stomach. Tears filled her eyes as she broke out in a sweat – and burped. This seemed to be the perfect reaction because Ho did a little jig. Apparently hugging was just for men.

Emily felt weak in the knees and knew the men were enjoying the show, but no one was going to escape unscathed. She turned and handed the flask to Long. The usually quiet, self-contained Ho was now hopping about with the joy of it all. He must be desperate for additional family members Emily thought wryly.

Long considered himself to be the outsider and was surprised to be included in the ritual. He suspected malicious intent on the part of Emily but was determined to step up to the occasion and acquit himself with honor – even though, unlike the others, he knew exactly what to expect. Long took the flask and swigged. It was everything he'd expected, but he'd done this many times before. Heck, he'd practically grown up on the stuff and had had plenty of opportunities to become accustomed. He was Vietnamese, after all, and this was a tradition of his culture. He smiled as he handed the flask back to Ho and received a hug for his efforts. As if to seal the deal, Ho took a drink, smacked his lips, burped and put the top back on. It seemed they were one, big happy family now.

The rice wine ritual warmed them in more ways than one and was a welcome conclusion to a near catastrophic day. When the tents were finally up, they were all out cold before they hit their mats. All except for Tom, who was checking to make sure the lighter was still there. He panicked when it wasn't where he usually kept it in his left-hand pocket, but a quick check of the right and he breathed again. Thank goodness for deep pockets, he muttered to himself as he drifted off.

It was the lighter that had brought him back to this deadly place. He had a score to settle and a promise to keep. The question this time was almost the same as the time before: was the mountain going to conquer him, or was he going to conquer it?

***

"Bravo Company is up front in pretty much constant and heavy contact with the enemy. They are organized and well equipped, so HQ thinks we're up against NVA soldiers," Skoberne explained as the men moved up toward the sound of gunfire. "Echo company is going in to support our men, take back the initiative and build up some momentum in this attack, " he continued.

"You got the lucky lighter?" Eddie asked.

"You know it," Skoberne said, producing it from his pocket, knowing his men had come to value it as much as their lieutenant did.

"All right then, let's go to war!" Eddie shouted, locking eyes with Tom.

Tom pushed forward with his head down, his hunched outline recognizable to anyone who had ever fought in a war with rifles. He had been in many small firefights, but in the last few days, he'd been involved in the biggest and most dangerous contacts of his tour. There was nothing in his past experience to compare with his present situation, but right now, he felt as if he was running into the maw of an angry colossus, and he was terrified. There were so many guns firing, so many bullets flying, surely one of them would find him. He tried not to think about himself as a victim, tried to think instead of the power he held in his hands. He clutched his M16, safety off, locked and loaded. It was wartime, and he was going to do everything he could to rain down fire and fury on the enemy. Every time he stole a glance at the other men in his squad, he saw hard faces and eyes in tight focus, everyone single-minded in anticipation of the fight ahead. The landscape was starting to widen, and the gradient was less severe. There was some room for maneuver but not much.

They were moving past some burnt-out hooches, the remnants of the first clash with the NVA, when a burst of heavy caliber machine gunfire whizzed overhead. Tom instinctively ducked but knew it was pointless; by the time you heard the bullet, you would have been hit if you were in its path. When the entire squad dived behind a gigantic moss-covered boulder, they found a couple of men from Bravo company already there. "The gooks have got us pretty much pinned down. Fortunately, they've got nothing to get through stone," Specialist Morrison observed.

Tom put his helmet on top of his rifle barrel and raised it above the edge of the rock. Seconds later, shots rang out and clanged against the metal. One of the bullets had ripped through his camouflage and torn the word 'Land' from his hand-drawn design of 'In Another Land'. "Shit!" Tom exclaimed, more than a little annoyed at the damage to his handiwork.

"Has anybody called in air support?" Zielinski asked.

"No, sir," Morrison replied.

Zielinski grabbed the handset from Ortiz's radio and began radioing in coordinates of a strike. He warned that the Americans were 'danger close' to the enemy and advised that the pilots needed to pick their targets carefully to avoid friendly-fire casualties.

The men hunkered down as they waited for the air force to do its thing. After a few minutes, there was a sound of distant thunder, which turned into the snarl of four huge propellor engines. An AC-130 Spectre hung impossibly in the air. It was on the hunt and it smelled blood.

The rumble of the giant aircraft was suddenly accompanied by a roar of fire as nearly 1,000 rounds a second tore through the jungle cover, and scores of 7.62 bullets cracked and skittered off the boulder the men were hiding behind. "Jesus, that's close," Tom shouted out, curling up in a ball trying to reduce his chances of being hit by the lethal metal torrent that poured down on the battlefield below the circling behemoth.

Cries could be heard over the sound of the fire from the Spectre, and not all of them were Vietnamese. The air cover lasted barely a minute and yet, in that time, over 40,000 rounds of ammunition had rained down on the ridgeline.

"The gooks are everywhere," the pilot of the gunship radioed into Zielinski.

"No shit! It's FUBAR," he muttered under his breath.

Tom spied Doc McCarrick running toward them, red in the face and breathing hard. "Get down, Doc," he cried out. The medic ignored him and was about to run past when Eddie grabbed him and brought him down behind the bolder. "Listen, Doc, I know you want to get to the wounded out there but stay behind the guys with guns. Let's face it, if you get zapped, who's going to patch you up?"

"Hell, who's going to patch the rest of us up?" Zielinski asked with a sardonic smile.

The doctor acquiesced and crouched down. Zielinski barked out orders, and the soldiers moved out from either side of the boulder, firing at any muzzle flashes they saw. They were soon joined by the rest of the platoon as they moved up to a nest of G.I.s who'd been caught in the firestorm. Some of them lay in silence, dead before their time; others flailed and writhed, their wounds like petals of flesh overflowing with the nectar of blood. Despite their obvious torment, they clung to their young lives with every breath, not willing to let go. The extent of their wounds could only have come from the Spectre. Had the air support done more harm than good? It was hard to say. Three companies of American soldiers had linked up in the remote hills of southern Vietnam, but they weren't making any forward progress.

Eddie's M60 barked at a nearby group of enemy soldiers, barely visible shapes in the tufts of elephant grass. Tom handed him another belt of ammunition. Skoberne darted from cover to cover to explain that they were going to remain on the hilltop overnight. The men were to dig in, and Claymores were to be set for a potential counter-attack by the NVA. This was by far the worst fighting Tom had ever been in.

The mood by dusk was grim, and the men were at their most vulnerable: covered in red dirt, baked in sweat, riddled with bug bites, weary of climbing and exhausted by the tension. Cold rations were little comfort, but no fires were lit so as to give nothing away to enemy snipers. Tom saw Eddie wiping his eyes. He had been straining them all day, trying to find enemy targets; now they were aching and watery. Looking past Eddie, Tom caught sight of Mo glancing at his pocket Bible. In the current situation maybe he could say a prayer for all of them.

Ortiz was rarely seen without the radio, but he had put it down and created a little nest for the two of them. He stayed close to this vital piece of equipment so as not to miss any messages coming in from command, from other field radios and from the air force, which would occasionally announce another run to spray the unseen enemy with high explosives or napalm.

Fire from the other side was sporadic, not enough to be considered an assault, but there were no long periods of calm either. Tom presumed they were conserving their ammo. As the sun went down over the crest of the mountains, darkness hid their positions from prying eyes but also increased the chance of a night attack. Bursts of gunfire made sleep impossible.

Tom was glad the Claymores, with their strangely reassuring 'front toward enemy' stamped on them, were in place to provide a nasty surprise for any potential attackers. Without a blanket of insulating cloud above them, the night turned cold when the wind picked up. Tom and Eddie stayed close in their shallow dugout, trying to preserve body heat, their thoughts running parallel. The bond they forged in wartime would keep them close for the rest of their lives, but right now they were drained by the intensity of their efforts to catch any sign of approaching enemy. Every fiber of their being strained to its limits. Were those shadows moving in the breeze enemy soldiers? Was that the noise of an animal or NVA? Did that cough come from an American or a Vietnamese?

The night spread its black cloak over friend and foe alike. Slivers of moonlight made specters of everyone. This was purgatory, the land between the living and the dead. Men lay down beside their sleeping comrades only to discover later that they weren't asleep but dead from previously unrecognized wounds. Here, the living rubbed shoulders with the dead; the line between the two became blurred, and sometimes no one knew the difference.

"This is some serious shit we're in," Eddie whispered to Tom after what felt like an eternity of silence.

"Yeah, we've really stepped on a hornet's nest this time," agreed Tom, who had been thinking along the same lines.

"Hornets with AKs and RPGs," Eddie replied with gallows' humor.

"Enemy contact!" yelled a soldier somewhere to their right, and flares were fired to illuminate the area ahead of the Americans. The flickering lights cast a surreal glow over the surrounding landscape and revealed that scores of NVA had moved forward silently and were about to overwhelm the front line.

The Claymores were detonated, and thousands of steel ball bearings ripped through dozens of enemy soldiers. A cloud of dust and blood obscured the view before the fallout from the mines could be revealed. Men lay strewn along the front, their bodies splayed in surreal positions. Bloody wounds, black in the night, blossomed over young men's bodies. A few writhed and cried out, but most were now corpses.

The Americans didn't hesitate and started to fire. The men were careful not to waste ammo, picking targets revealed by the flares, shooting at muzzle flashes and the sound of padding footsteps. All were legitimate targets in the dead of night. Eddie blasted away, and Tom joined in as enemy soldiers attempted to rush them and get into their lines. There was the whoosh, fizz and then the detonation of an RPG, fired by an invisible enemy. The NVA had bayonets fixed, and they screamed as they charged toward the G.I.s, the Claymores doing little to stop an overwhelming onrush. Despite the furious firing from the three companies of American soldiers, the Vietnamese were able to close and engage. There were screams as men fell under furious blasts of gunfire or felt cold steel slicing through their warm flesh.

Between Eddie's machine gun blasting away whole belts of ammo, and Mo's shotgun taking down anything in a twenty-yard radius, Tom's squad created a makeshift safe zone that other soldiers gravitated to. Tom took off the two belts of 7.62 ammo for Eddie to use. A soldier leaped down beside Eddie and Tom, startling both of them. Tom looked up to see the dead eyes of Humby who wore a strangely joyous grin; he was holding something in his hand. "I got myself another ear," he said, waving a slice of blood-drenched flesh in his hand. "I'm gonna add it to my collection, but this one is special. These dinks are wearing uniforms; I got me my first NVA ear," Humby said, grinning in awe at the piece of another human being, torn from a corpse.

Under the circumstances, Tom wondered if the psychopath standing next to him was a greater threat than the enemy around him. "That's great, Humby," lied Tom. "Why don't you see if you can go get some more." Humby's eyes sparkled. "Good thinking, Moretti," Humby said, patting Tom on the shoulder with the hand that held the ear and dripping blood onto his flak jacket. Humby tucked the ear in a pocket and crept off into the shadows.

Eddie stopped firing for a moment. "That cat scares the shit out of me," Eddie said, shaking his head.

"I think I'm glad he's on our side," Tom replied. He went back to peering down his iron sight as both of them continued their search for fresh targets.

***

The creeping rays of sunrise bathed the tent in light, causing Tom to stir from his restless sleep. He rubbed his eyes and made his way out to a breathtakingly beautiful morning. He walked closer to the cliff edge to answer a call of nature and wondered why he hadn't seen this magnificent scenery all those years ago. Of course, his focus as a soldier had been different; the priority then was scanning the area for any signs of the enemy. No one cared about 'the view'. Afterward, back home, his memories of the jungle were full of fear and danger and a desperate desire to get out. Now, with the help of time, his older eyes could see that Vietnam must be one of the lushest places on the planet, a place his nation had bombed and napalmed until it was a scorched landscape. The land had recovered and thrived. The Vietnamese people seemed to have done the same. Could he?

His thoughts were interrupted by Long, who joined him with a cheery good morning as he took care of his own needs a little distance away.

By this time Emily was up and regarded the two men with mild disdain. Men, to them the whole world is a bathroom, she thought as she headed down the path to find a suitable bush. Unfortunately the bush she chose already had an occupant, and she jumped when Ho emerged with his usual grin on a sun-crinkled face. "Men!" she shouted and stormed back up the hill, still looking for a piece of privacy. Ho didn't understand her obvious irritation, chalked it up to more puzzling American behavior and headed back to their hasty encampment where he was, almost miraculously, brewing tea. Somehow he had found the means to start a fire, no small achievement, given everything was wet.

As they prepared to set off again, Tom approached Long who was packing away his things. "Last night was pretty damn scary."

Long laughed nervously. "Yes, it was, for all of us."

"I feel awful about what happened to Ho. Could you come with me and translate?" Long nodded and they made their way over to Ho, who made it clear it was time to get going.

"I feel responsible for what happened last night," Tom began and paused while Long translated. Now it was Tom's turn to give Ho a little speech, and Ho listened politely but impassively.

"This trip, ah, journey, whatever you want to call it, this is about me and my past. I feel bad enough that I've dragged my granddaughter into it, but you and Long don't owe me anything. Way I figure, you might well have had a better life if my country had acted differently half a century ago. Same goes for Long. And then last night, you nearly died and Long's life was in jeopardy too, all because you're both helping me on this selfish journey."

"I could have backed out at any time; it was my decision to come," Long said. He translated everything for Ho who indicated he agreed with Long. They were here by choice.

"I appreciate that, but I can no longer take responsibility for your safety. Long is in the midst of family life; me, I'm at the end of mine. I can afford to take chances, but I have no right to involve either of you in this, and I want you to know that I am sorry for all that's happened."

"I wouldn't be here if I didn't want to help," Long replied.

"And for that, Long, I have no idea how to repay you, but this is as far as you go. I'm not sure what's up there on the summit, but I do know that while I'm willing to take risks to get there, you and Ho have done more than enough."

Long dropped his head while he considered how to respond. "To be honest, I am not here just for you. I know it started out that way, but that was before Emily was part of the picture. I am worried about the split that has developed between the two of you. I know that this is not my business, but I don't want to leave you both stranded out here – and I'm not just talking about physically."

"I know what you're saying, but from here on in, Emily and I have to figure it out," Tom said firmly. "But before you go, there's something I have to tell you; it's a confession," Tom said, looking now only at Long, who said nothing, waiting to hear what Tom would say.

From her position in the bushes, Emily was able to listen in on the conversation. She hardly dared to breathe, worried that any interruption would break the spell.

"When we met in the park, you wondered why I was staring at your mother's apartment building. I didn't tell you at the time, but I was reliving the day when I was part of the squad that brought the war to her home. I was ashamed that we had given no thought to the civilian occupants of that building, ashamed that I had a role in her near death. Now I'm ashamed that it has taken me so long to tell you this."

Long reached over and placed his hand on Tom's shoulder, saying, "Thank you for telling me. I had guessed as much, but it was up to you to tell me in your own time. My mother harbors no ill feeling toward the Americans and neither do I. But ... I try not to think how my life would have been different if the Americans hadn't lost."

Even though their relationship could be measured only in days, Tom knew that Long had become a key part of everything his journey represented; he was the link between the old and the new. He had somehow realized that was his role, but now Tom needed to find his own path between these two worlds. "Thank you for being more than a guide and a translator. Thank you for being my friend," Tom said, his voice trembling with emotion.

Long didn't trust himself to speak, so he just nodded.

"We've spent enough time in my past. It's time for you to go back to your family."

"What about Ho? Won't you need a guide?"

"No, I know the summit can't be far away, and as for the return journey … well, good thing we weren't trying to hide our trail; it's obvious enough for a child to track us. We'll just follow it back.

"Here," Tom said, reaching into his pack and bringing out a fistful of notes. "I know I already paid you, but this is something extra, for your trouble and Ho's."

Long looked at the notes. It was probably the equivalent of two weeks' wages, but it would be wrong to take it. "Thank you, but I cannot."

"It would make me happy if you would," Tom coaxed, knowing Long was too polite to take it on the first offer.

"I can't," Long replied but indicated Ho should be consulted.

Tom turned to Ho, saying, "You need to take this. Use it to help the village. Dig a new well or something."

Just then, Emily stepped out of the bushes, surprising them all. "That's a great idea, Grandpa. I've been thinking and I have decided I'd like to stay in the village and put my skills to use there. Your money, plus what I have, will help set up a small clinic and buy some much-needed medical supplies."

Long could hardly believe what he was hearing. "Two worlds collide and a new generation helps heal the old," he mused out loud. The money would have immediate benefits for the health of the villagers. It was a wonderful gesture – and the fact that Emily would stay on to work with them would make all the difference. Long quickly explained the plan to Ho, who burst out laughing and chattering.

When Long translated, he did so with a smile. "Ho says he was right to make you members of his family. This is what families do for each other." Long paused. "He also said, 'Enough talking, let's get going!'"

Tom handed the money over to Ho, who bowed graciously to Tom and then to Emily before grabbing his staff and heading off down the path. Long signaled that he'd catch up in a minute.

"I will need your help with translation, so I'll 'Friend' you on Facebook," Emily said to Long. Her mind was now working overtime on a plan that was still forming. "I want to create a closed group and get my friend Jessica involved, too. She can help raise more money and source medical supplies. This might even get her to come out. I'll lie and tell her Vietnamese Cheerios are better than the American ones."

Long wasn't sure what the last comment meant, but he understood the overall plan. He told Emily she could count on him and that he'd visit the village when he could get away.

"It's good to know we have friends … family … in Vietnam," Tom said with a chuckle. He was still taking in Emily's pronouncements. The girl had changed and the changes were dramatic. She had a plan and she was determined.

Even so, she was young and it would give him peace of mind to know that Long and Ho were nearby. They were family after all.

Long picked up his pack and said to Tom, "You are like America, you do everything with a big heart. Sometimes you get it wrong, but what you do comes from a good place. I don't know what's waiting for you on that summit, but whatever it is, I hope you make peace with your past – as well as with your present." This time, Tom could only nod in agreement.

Long bowed and said, "*Vạn sự như ý*". Neither Tom nor Emily had a clue what it meant, but they bowed in return and watched Long walk away, running a little to catch up with Ho. They turned for one last wave goodbye, and then they were gone.

"Right," said a determined Tom. "Let's get to the top of this ridge."

***

The Americans came under regular attacks throughout the night. It was estimated that thirty-five men had been carried down to the base below, either for medevac or body bags. Tom and his squad had grabbed only minutes of fretful sleep and were exhausted by the almost constant combat. As dawn broke, Tom was still reflecting on earlier events. He was in a deadly situation, but he had killed a child. He wanted desperately to live, but he didn't think he deserved to. This fight up the ridgeline was surely his punishment, but how would it end? For him, for all of them, it didn't look good.

Tom stared down at his dirt-stained hands with thick curves of black filth under his fingernails. His clothes were drenched in sweat and muck. He probably smelled as bad as he looked, but he couldn't tell. He felt as if he had become the physical embodiment of war, of its terror, agony and bloodshed, but he was no commander, no general; he was just a scared kid, sick to his stomach with what he had seen and done. He wanted to go home and soak in the bath for days; he wanted to wash away his sins and feel the love and comfort of family. He wanted peace but feared it would always be denied him, the price for all he had done.

Zielinski slid in beside Tom and Eddie. "The air force is going to hit the gooks with some ordinance, and that will be our signal to push forward. If they are putting up such fierce resistance, they have to be protecting something valuable. So we are pushing on."

The stern order snapped Tom back to the present. He had the job of soldiering to do. If his mistakes cost him his life, so be it. But if his mistakes cost the life of Eddie or any of his squadmates, Tom knew there was a special place in hell for soldiers who failed their brothers-in-arms. "Yes, sir," Tom and Eddie replied together.

A few minutes later and a new sound filled the air. Up until now, everything that had flown in had been propeller driven, but now they saw the sleek outlines of two Super Sabre jets, flying low and level. Tom instinctively tilted his helmet a little further forward to protect himself from the coming blast. The fighters released napalm pods that tumbled silently in the air before exploding in a roar of orange flames across the land and the enemy in front of them.

Tom heard a few cheers from some of the men around him. He just hoped the strike was enough to clear the path ahead. They waited a few minutes for the inferno to subside but not so long as to allow the enemy to regroup.

"Go! Go! Go!" Zielinski barked and moved forward, the rest of the men following closely behind. They rushed into the thick black smoke that had not only roasted the enemy front line but acted as a screen for the advancing Americans. Tom saw several NVA bodies lying on the ground engulfed in flames. The smell of petroleum and burning wood was accompanied by a sweeter smell almost like roast pork, which Humby had told him was human flesh, and if anybody knew what that smelled like, it would be him.

The men were making good progress as they pushed on uphill. 100 yards and no contact, 200 yards and nothing still. Had the planes killed the last of them? Had the soldiers whittled down the enemy to almost nothing and then the air force finished the job? At 250 yards there was a burst of gunfire, and Tom hit the ground, cursing under his breath. Of course there were more of them. Charlie, the jungle, even fate would not let him off that easily.

Tom fired off a few shots in the general direction of the sound of gunfire, but the smoke and flames completely obscured his vision. He looked to his left and saw Skoberne and Ortiz hunched by a burning tree stump as they radioed in the current situation. Then he heard the crack and sizzle of 7.62 rounds coming dangerously close.

"11 o'clock, 60 yards," Eddie shouted to Tom as he set up his M60 ready to fire.

Tom focused in and saw a man with an AK47, lying prone, not far away. He squeezed the trigger of his rifle and hit the NVA soldier in the temple and shoulder. The man went limp and dropped his weapon. The exchange of gunfire erupted in a deafening sound. Tom had never understood why the M16 had a 20 bullet magazine versus the AKs 30. They had to reload a third of the time more frequently, and in a battle like this, that was a definite disadvantage.

Tom ejected an empty magazine and reached into his pack, just two left. The fighting had been so heavy that while he hadn't wasted ammo, he was running low. He slapped in a new mag and turned to Eddie. "How many belts have you got left?"

Eddie patted the one on his chest and looked around. "The one in the pig and the one I'm carrying and that's it. The way I'm going, I'll be done in the next hour," Eddie said with a look of concern.

Tom scrambled over to Skoberne. "Sir, I've only got two full mags left, and Eddie on the 60 has got a belt and a half, and then he's out."

Skoberne nodded. "ARVN troops are coming up from behind to resupply."

"It's about time they did some of the heavy lifting."

"That it is."

"Incoming!" came a shout of warning as mortar rounds flew into the air.

Tom instinctively rolled away from Skoberne into a nearby recess in the cliff face. The mortar shells landed with a loud thud and detonated. One was close enough that the pressure wave threw dirt and debris into Tom's eyes. It took a moment for him to blink away the grit and tears - and then he saw Skoberne and Ortiz. The mortar round had detonated next to them. Tom rushed over and saw the bloody mess.

Skoberne's eyelids were already drooping over glassy eyes. Most of his lower abdomen had been torn off and blood poured out of his brutalized body. He coughed up blood. "Moretti, don't let those bastards win this one."

"No, sir," Tom said, looking into the eyes of a dying man. He could see Skoberne's light ebbing away in front of him.

"Top left pocket," Skoberne spluttered through the blood in his throat.

Tom's hands fumbled with the button, his fingers thick with mud and blood. He reached in and found the Zippo lighter with the regimental insignia on the front, Skoberne's company, platoon and name on the back.

"It's the lucky lighter … guess my luck's run out … I want to be with you guys when you get to the top … My way of beating Charlie … bury it up there …"

Tom looked down at the lighter. It was his lieutenant's favorite possession, the platoon's good luck charm and a symbol of the bond of brotherhood forged in the inferno of war. But most importantly, it was the dying wish of a good man. "I promise, sir," Tom said with tears in his eyes. When he looked back at Skoberne, his head was lolling to one side, the light in his eyes had gone out. Had he heard Tom promise? No matter, Tom had made the promise and had every intention of honoring it.

Tom looked down and saw that he was kneeling in a pool of his lieutenant's blood. It felt disrespectful so he moved away and over to the groaning Ortiz. The heavy radio pack had taken some of the blast, but from knee to shoulder, the man's left side was lacerated and bleeding.

"Santa Maria, esto duele!" Ortiz cried out as he writhed on the ground.

The shadow of Tom's figure fell across his face and Ortiz looked up. "How bad is it, Moretti?"

Tom crouched down to inspect the wounds. Ortiz saw the worried look on his face and sobbed, "Ah Jesus, man, I don't wanna die!"

"Medic! Somebody get the doc now!" Tom bellowed. "You're not gonna die, Ortiz. Help is coming."

The response to his desperate cry was met with random shouts and gunfire. "Medic! Medic!" Tom shouted again and again.

If anyone heard him, no one was in a position to reply. The noise of fighting continued all around. Tom looked down at Ortiz who was bleeding heavily and starting to go pale in the face. The wounds didn't seem too serious, but there were so many of them, and he was losing a lot of blood.

Tom looked at the lighter in his hand, remembering the promise he had just made, and quickly stashed it in his pocket. Then he fumbled for both his and Ortiz's medical kits. He'd just lost Skoberne; he wasn't planning on losing Ortiz as well. He got out the pressure bandages and tourniquets. He hadn't used either since basic training, but he had to do something to stop the bleeding. He put the first tourniquet around Ortiz's thigh. He cried out in pain.

"Sorry, man," apologized Tom.

"No, do what you have to do to keep me alive," Ortiz said through gritted teeth.

Tom applied a second tourniquet high up on Ortiz's left arm. Then he applied one pressure bandage to Ortiz's abdomen and another to his hip. He pulled back to look at his work. There was blood everywhere, and he was covered in it, but there was nothing else he could do. Only medics carried painkillers; all he had done was buy Ortiz some time. "I'm gonna go find Doc and get him over here ASAP."

Ortiz grabbed Tom's flak jacket with his good hand. "Don't leave me here. I don't want to die alone in this stinking country."

"I have to get help or you're gonna bleed out."

Ortiz groaned, "Okay, Moretti, but please don't let me die out here on this worthless, goddam hillside."

Tom nodded and ran off, thinking about the good men who were dying on this worthless, goddam hillside. What was so special about this place? When they got to the top, all the blood, all the corpses had better be worth it. Tom darted from foxhole to tree stump in his search for a medic. Eventually, he found Doc McCarrick administering morphine to a soldier who had taken several rounds to the chest. The soldier was propped up behind a tree stump, unconscious.

"Is he still alive?" Tom said, staring at the state of his wounds.

"Unbelievably, yes. But I can't move him or he definitely will die."

"Doc, I need you to come with me. A mortar round killed Lieutenant Skoberne and seriously wounded Ortiz."

"Skoberne is dead?" McCarrick asked, stunned by the news.

"Yes, took a direct hit from a mortar."

"No! He was a good man."

"Yes, he was, but you have to come with me now or we're going to lose another one."

"Right you are, son. You lead on, I'm right behind you."

Tom darted from cover to cover but realized Doc, a middle-aged man, was slower, so he gave him covering fire as they moved along. There was another cry for a medic. Doc paused and looked around.

"No, you don't, Doc. I got you first. Keep going and keep your head down."

McCarrick replied with a nod, and the two men made their way along the row of American soldiers until they found their way back to Skoberne and Ortiz. McCarrick looked down at Skoberne's broken body and whispered, "Dear God". Then he turned to Ortiz whose eyes were closed. Had he bled out on the battlefield? Had Tom let him down? Doc started by checking his pulse.

"Is he alive?" Tom asked anxiously.

McCarrick looked up from his work and glared at Tom. "Dammit, do you have any idea how hard it is to check a wounded man's pulse when there is shooting all around you?"

"No," Tom said sheepishly.

"It's pretty damn hard, so I don't need any interruptions, alright private?"

"Yes, sir."

Doc went back to looking for a pulse and smiled. "Well, it's faint, but it's there. You did a good job with the bandages and tourniquets. Without them, he would be dead for sure."

Tom sighed with relief.

"He needs to get a medevac ASAP. Get him to the rear so the ARVN troops can take him down to the LZ."

"Yes, sir!" This was an order Tom could happily follow. It felt like a moment of redemption. All he had done for months was kill and destroy, but this was about keeping someone alive. Nothing could wash away the blood he had on his hands, but to help save the life of a squadmate was a duty that felt right for a change. He scanned the area, a fractured scene of muzzle flashes, smoke, vegetation and men sprawled on the ground, fighting or dying. Tom needed help and his eyes fell on Mo, crouching behind a small mound of dirt and grass. He scrabbled toward him, ignoring the rifle fire all around, and hit the ground next to Mo. "Are you crazy, white boy?" Mo scolded him.

"It's the lieutenant and Ortiz," Tom spat out. Mo saw the look on Tom's face and realized it was bad.

"What happened?"

"They took a mortar round. Lieutenant Skoberne is dead, but Ortiz, he's hurt and unconscious. I need you to help me get him to medevac."

Mo nodded and pointed for Tom to lead the way. They darted back to where Ortiz lay. Doc had moved on, but before he did he had taken Skoberne's poncho out and laid it over his body. Under the circumstances, it was all anyone could do.

Tom held the unconscious Ortiz under the arms, Mo picked up his legs, and they began to move carefully down the hillside. They heard a few cracks of gunfire but nothing more. It was as if the monster of war was prowling around, looking for prey and found them to be of little interest. Luckily for them, its greedy eyes were fixed on other targets.

As they moved away from the front line, the sounds of war grew weaker, faint echoes in the jungle as some of the blasts bounced off the canopy. Moving the dead weight of Ortiz was hard work, and both men took care not to jolt him for fear of doing more harm than good getting him to a chopper. They knew that had the tables been turned, Ortiz would do the same for them.

As they picked their way through rough terrain, they heard Ortiz groaning, and they stared at each other with identical looks of anxiety. They paused and set Ortiz down gently. Tom pulled out his canteen and gulped down some water.

"May I? I'm out," Mo said. Tom, his cheeks, bulging with chemically treated water, handed the canteen over to Mo, who took a hefty swig and handed it back. "Thanks, there's still a little bit left." Then, "That canteen is a lot like our ammo situation, " Mo said bluntly as they prepared to set off again.

"I thought I was the only one running low. I'm hoping when we get to the ARVN troops they can take Ortiz and give us some ammo."

"Sounds like a plan, my man," Mo said with a grunt as he braced himself to take the weight of Ortiz's legs.

The two of them lifted together and continued down the path. The battle, now above them, sounded like a far-off storm. In the distance, they could see the village where they'd been so recently. The charred remnants of hooches reminded Tom again of what he had done there ... as if he could forget.

Meanwhile, overhead, Hueys came whining into the area, touched down and, in a matter of minutes, lifted off again. Tom and Mo headed down into the jungle canopy where they found ARVN troops ready and waiting. The two men carefully placed Ortiz on a stretcher and he was carried from their sight. Ortiz would survive in a coma but eventually be declared brain dead in 1970, when his life support was switched off.

Mixing with the ARVN troops were a number of American soldiers, mainly stretcher bearers and medical personnel. Tom spotted some of them heading uphill, empty-handed. "Hey, fellas," Tom called out.

"What?" came a testy reply.

"We're running low on ammo. If you're going back up, take some up with you."

"It's not our job," complained one of them.

"So fucking what? You want us to start throwing rocks at the dinks?" shouted Mo, putting his shotgun on his shoulder to underline his point.

The soldier sighed, shrugged and returned down the hillside, all in one smooth movement of compliance. The others followed.

"Thank you, kindly," Mo said, the comment dripping with sarcasm, which was lost on its target.

The stretcher bearers loaded up with piles of ammo while Mo and Tom each opened a 7.62 ammo box and put belts of M60 ammunition across their chests. After replenishing their own supplies, they each grabbed two boxes of rifle ammo and filled their canteens. They were starting up the hill again when there was a sudden burst of automatic gunfire close by. The NVA had sent a battalion of fresh troops into the rear of the American force. Both Tom and

Mo knew the ARVN were not up to the task of stopping such a large, well-trained and highly motivated force.

Tom saw the stretcher bearers looking bewildered as they set down their burdens and considered what to do. "Keep going! If the rest of the guys are going to have to fight their way off these hills, they'll need that ammo!" Tom bellowed at them. The men nodded and started back up the trail with their precious cargo.

Tom ran to the medical personnel. While Tom and Mo were some of the lowest ranked personnel in the area, they were the only battle-hardened frontline troops. "Everyone find cover. Medics, this is the time to put down your bandages and grab a rifle." Tom turned to an ARVN captain. "Your men have to hold this position or the three companies of Americans up there are going to be surrounded, you got that?" The captain nodded and began issuing orders in Vietnamese.

The exchanges of gunfire were intense. An ARVN soldier threw a smoke grenade. "What the fuck do you think you're doing?" Mo bellowed at the man. "Now we can't see the enemy, so they'll sneak up and get closer."

The Vietnamese soldier looked confused and ashamed. Mo realized he couldn't speak English but understood that his action had incurred the wrath of a big, black American clutching a shotgun. Tom and Mo ran from one group of bewildered soldiers to another to secure the perimeter. Combat troops they were not, but their comrades up in the clouds were depending on them to give them an escape route.

An NVA soldier came screaming out of nowhere, clutching his AK47 like a melee weapon, it's sharp steel bayonet ready to pierce the chest of an enemy soldier. Mo brought his Stevens Model 77E up and fired at point-blank range, blowing the man off his feet with one blast from his shotgun. Mo pointed to three members of the medical corps. "Do that," he said simply. The men looked at their Browning pistols and M14 rifles despondently. "Mine is different, but they're all guns; you point them and you shoot them. Remember that from basic?" Mo roared at them.

Tom discovered a heavy weapons' team had just arrived with a .30 cal heavy machine gun. He helped them find a spot that could give them the maximum firing arc and brought up some extra ammo for them. "Remember, you have to buy us time to get our guys off that ridgeline. Got it?"

"Yes, sir," one of the men said, mistaking Tom for someone of a more senior rank.

Tom ducked back, dodging incoming fire to find Mo. "What do you think?"

"I think one of us has to stay here to help these men grow some balls."

"Alright, you stay here. I'll take some ammo up and make sure that the message has been passed along that we have to get off these damn hills."

"Deal," Mo said bluntly.

Tom grabbed two boxes of ammo and was heading back up the track when Mo called out to him, "And just remember who saved your sorry white ass."

"My sorry white ass thanks you," Tom countered and began to jog up the hill. It was the second time he'd had to climb this cursed track. As he picked his way over loose debris, he came across wounded men heading down. Some were on stretchers; others were walking wounded trussed up in bandages, blood slowly spreading over their white dressings. This was not good. They had been thrown into a meat grinder, and they had nothing to show for their efforts. But now was not the time for anger and remorse. These had to be pushed aside for the greater priority of helping his platoon escape the hell that was theirs right now.

Tom caught up with the stretcher bearers who were plodding up the path. "You guys are carrying ammo that will save American lives. You get that, right?" Tom snapped. The men looked blankly at him. "So get moving! Lives depend on it."

"We're doing our best, but it's heavy," whined one of them.

"Hey, I'm sorry to hear that. The war has been a real inconvenience to me too, but you know what? The guys fighting up there need this shit, so pull your fingers out and get moving!"

Tom scrambled on ahead of them but eventually had to pause to catch his breath. Even though he was young and in the best shape of his life, he was pushing himself to his physical limits. He had been in four major contacts in three days, had had no decent sleep for days, and now he was carrying heavy ammo up a steep hill in tropical conditions. He put the ammo down and sat on the ground, his forge-like lungs gulping in air, his heart pounding in his ears. Sweat poured off him. He opened his flak jacket to allow some kind of cooling and drained the water from his canteen. He was giving himself another minute to allow his body to cool when the stretcher bearers caught up with him. That was his cue to move. Ignoring the struggling men, he zipped up his body armor, picked up the ammo and kept pushing on.

***

Tom put down his pack and sat on the ground, his forge-like lungs gulping in air, his heart pounding in his ears. Sweat poured off him. He was old and the trail was hard. The only cure to growing old was to die young and he had somehow avoided that. His actions on that day fifty years ago had earned him a Bronze Star for bravery, but he always thought it should have gone to men like Skoberne, though what good medals were when you were dead he didn't know – anymore than he knew what good they were when you were alive. He had acted instinctively for the good of everyone. That's what you did in the army. Maybe, for him, it was also the chance for a little piece of redemption. God knew a helluva lot of what they all did was beyond redemption – it was inhumane and it was immoral – but it was the army and it was war. It's just that he didn't need the army and its medals to tell him he was good or right or brave.

Emily was about ten paces ahead of him when she looked back and saw her grandfather sitting on a low bank next to the trail. She walked back to him and put her own pack on the ground. "Are you okay, Grandpa?" she asked with some concern.

Tom had spent the morning telling her what had happened on this ridgeline all those years ago. Emily had listened intently and had even asked questions. It was the most conversation they'd had for days. He didn't want to push it, but he had to hope this was a sign that relations between them were thawing.

The stories of the Americans' seeming indifference to civilians had caused Emily the most pain. His involvement in the killing of women and children had shaken her to her core. But now he had told her the story of one army fighting another and, while she knew this is what war had always been about, she realized how close her grandfather had come to death on numerous occasions. It was chilling. And it was selfish. Had Private First Class Thomas Enrico Moretti died on this slope, he would never have married her grandmother, and she would never have existed. It was sobering. When she thought of the young men in her life, she couldn't begin to imagine them in her grandfather's situation. Their biggest concerns were wi-fi connections or the ethical sourcing of their coffee. What her grandfather described happening on this mountain was primal, a battle for survival against terrible odds.

As she trudged along, she had reflected that for her generation, it was her grandfather's that had screwed over the world and left them with a mess to sort out. Global warming, economic crises, unresolved conflicts everywhere were their legacy. But then again, hadn't her grandfather and the youth of his generation been the victims of the mistakes of those who had preceded them? After all, a teen from Illinois didn't start the Vietnam War. Maybe it had always been this way, each generation coping with the mistakes of their forefathers, thinking they could do better, until they realized too late that they, too, were leaving a poisoned legacy for the next one.

"I guess the years have caught up with me," Tom sighed, still gulping air.

Emily crouched down, pushed her cool Ray-Bans onto her forehead and leaned over for a closer look. Her grandfather was wet through with sweat, breathing hard and bright pink in the face. The exertions in the mountains were too much for his aging body, and she was worried that he might have a heart attack or stroke. What would she do? No phone and the village was more than two days away. She pulled her sunglasses back down over her eyes, hoping he couldn't see the anxiety she was feeling.

"You're looking a little hot and bothered," Emily said, painting on a smile.

Tom took off his baseball cap and fanned himself with it. "I'll be alright, just let me catch my breath."

With not much in the way of options, they sat for a while in silence, waiting for Tom to recover. For the first time on the trip, Emily felt close to him, felt as though the stories he shared were relevant to her and that, somehow, she had a stake in all this, too.

Looking back, from the moment her trip had been taken out of her hands that day over Easter dinner, she had been dreading it, and she had blamed her grandfather for everything. She was mad at him for hijacking her life and used that as an excuse to judge him for things she knew nothing about. In her pettiness, she had refused to even try to understand a man whose own life was in turmoil not only because he had lost his beloved wife, but because that loss had triggered painful memories, memories that had brought him here – with her. Even when she hadn't been looking, he had shown her things she could never have seen without him. Hadn't that been exactly what she had hoped for? Hadn't seeing new things and challenging herself been a goal of her travels? Her grandfather had always given her the chance to opt out of his plans, but she was beginning to think that he knew her well enough to understand that she would never back out. Had that also been part of his plan?

Her thoughts were interrupted. "You know, a lot of good men died here," Tom said, beginning to feel rested.

"Yes, Grandpa, nearly 60,000."

"No, I mean here on this ridge. When people start throwing around statistics like 60,000 dead, the numbers just don't mean anything. You have to bring the numbers alive, and for me, the numbers have stories. I was the one who stood over their bloody bodies. I was the one who looked into the eyes of a young officer who should have had his whole life ahead of him, but who died in front of me. Those numbers have faces and mangled bodies and mothers who will never stop weeping. I saw slaughter and carnage throughout my tour, but here, here was the worst. Here is where we were beaten." Tom paused and thought for a moment before adding, "In every sense of the word".

"Why was it so important? What's at the top?" Emily asked.

"Don't know, never got that far, but I have a promise to keep," Tom grunted as he got to his feet. He put his cap back on and adjusted it purposefully as he turned to his granddaughter. "Come on, let's find out."

***

Eddie saw a shadowy shape move out of cover about seventy yards in front of him. He squeezed the trigger of his M60 and let out a brief burst of fire. The figure dropped to the ground and an ominous silence followed. Eddie had been right on target, but now he was out of ammo. He turned to Zielinski. "I'm out," he said flatly.

"Me too, son, " Zielinski replied while waving his Browning M1911 automatic pistol. "But I've got this. It saved my ass in Korea and I have no doubt it'll save it again."

"I've been hearing what sounds like firefights coming from below us as well as in front. Is that just some kind of weird echo or something?"

"Negative. Charlie is trying to flank us and is hitting the ARVN troops in the rear," Zielinski said neutrally. Both of them knew this was bad news, but what was going to save the day was calm heads.

"We're gonna need ammo if we want to keep fighting."

"And it's on its way. We've got supplies coming up with men from the rear. Get your k-bar out, ready to use. Better to have that in your hand than your dick."

"I don't know about that, " Eddie said with a broad smile. "You haven't seen my dick."

"Don't want to, don't plan to," Zielinski retorted, patting Eddie on the shoulder. "Wait here. I'm going to see if I can find someone, anyone with ammo for the pig." Zielinski crept off, making sure to keep a low profile. He had seen the fear in Eddie's eyes, but the sergeant knew his men, and he knew Eddie was the joker of the squad. Set him up for a dick joke and, as expected, the Eddie they needed resurfaced. Zielinski smiled to himself. He wasn't a good staff sergeant because he was tough, he was good because he could read people and tell them what they needed to hear.

Eddie lay alongside his impotent machine gun. He wasn't alone in his need for ammo. American fire was sporadic as they now only shot at what they knew they could hit. The enemy must have sensed the tide was turning in their favor, and there was another assault on the American front line. The last of the Claymores was fired. Men screamed and fell, but far more rushed forward, foliage tied to their wide-brimmed helmets, their uniforms and webbing marking them out as substantially different to the peasant attire and equipment of the Viet Cong the Americans had been used to fighting.

The G.I.s opened up with everything they had. Eddie had an antipersonnel grenade in one hand and his k-bar in the other when he saw three men heading his way. He quickly put down the knife, pulled the pin of the grenade, waited for the second it took him to stand up and threw it in the direction of the NVA soldiers. It caught one on the collarbone, and he winced as the metal bruised him just before he caught sight of what it was. His eyes widened as he was engulfed in the blast. Eddie's grenade killed one man instantly and scythed through the body of the second. He went down and writhed on the ground as he bled out, but the blast had done nothing to stop the momentum of the third man who was now virtually on top of Eddie.

There was no time to pick up his knife as the enemy soldier came screaming toward him; his bayonet was fixed to his rifle, and his face was full of rage. Eddie reached out and grabbed at the barrel jacket behind the razor-sharp knife, trying to angle the weapon away from his body. When the two men crashed into each other, there was a burst of automatic fire from the rifle that tore angrily into the dirt to Eddie's right. The NVA soldier's momentum pushed Eddie backward off his feet as he tried to swing with his left at the man's face. His fist missed, but his elbow connected sharply with the bridge of the soldier's nose. Eddie felt it give as the man tumbled on top of him and tried to bring his gun to bear. The two were now rolling around on the ground in a vicious fight to the finish.

The NVA soldier pulled his rifle out of Eddie's grasp in a desperate frenzy. He brought the wooden stock down on Eddie, but the rim of his helmet saved him from a brutal concussion. The near miss threw the soldier off balance and slightly to the side so that when he rose to bring the butt of his AK down again, Eddie seized the opportunity to bring his leg up and knee him in the groin. The man crumpled.

Eddie looked frantically at his k-bar lying on the ground and reached over to grab it. The soldier recovered sufficiently to thrust his bayonet toward his opponent. Out of the corner of his eye, Eddie saw light reflecting off metal and watched in horrified fascination as the hard, unyielding steel punctured the back of his right hand. His fingers splayed in pain and, instinctively, he tugged foolishly against the bayonet, making his wound worse as he screamed in agony.

The enemy soldier pulled out his blade and brought the barrel of his gun around to finish Eddie. Despite his pain, Eddie's left hand grabbed the carry handle of the M60 and swung twenty-three pounds of solid metal into the shoulder of the NVA soldier, who finally fell off. Despite his agony, despite the fact that his grip on the gun was compromised by the slippery blood pumping from his own body, Eddie seized his machine gun in both hands, clutching it for all he was worth. With a primal scream of rage and pain, Eddie brought the butt of his M60 down on the man's face with all of his might. The blow fractured the soldier's skull, tore open the skin above his right eyebrow and knocked him senseless. Eddie roared a second time and brought the butt of his weapon down on the man's head again. And again and again and again, bludgeoning the man to death and spraying blood over everything, including himself.

Eddie fell back onto his heels, panting as the battle raged around him. He was alive. He had just survived his closest brush with death, and he was exhilarated. What lay in front of him was the bloody remains of a human being, and yet, the adrenaline coursing through his veins invigorated him.

It must be wrong to feel elated, but Eddie couldn't help it. The dead man wasn't a human being, he was a gook, a no-good dirty commie bastard. It was me against him thought Eddie. Only one of us could win this encounter, only one of us could survive it. Eddie was glad it was him.

He looked around for his first-aid kit and pulled out a bandage. He lay low, knowing he was vulnerable while he attended to his medical needs. He fumbled with the dressing as his right hand bled profusely over the white dressing, but eventually, he managed to stop the bleeding. When he looked up to see what was going on, the movement caught the eye of a nearby NVA soldier who was raising his rifle. Eddie reached desperately for the AK47 lying in the dirt nearby when two shots rang out, and two red sprays exploded in the front of the man's chest. He dropped to the ground with a look of confusion on his face. The shots had come from behind Eddie who turned to see Zielinski standing there, Browning in hand.

"I leave you for five minutes and you get yourself wounded. That's unacceptable, Powell."

"Yes, sir, sorry sir," Eddie said, trying to smile but wincing instead.

"What happened, son?"

"Bayonet through the hand. Got the sonofabitch though," Eddie said, nodding at the corpse.

Zielinski looked at the mangled head of the dead NVA soldier. "Yes, you did. What did you do, exactly, hit him with a buffalo?"

"As a matter of fact, it was a pig, sir."

Zielinski couldn't help himself and smiled. "Alright, soldier, I've spoken to Captain de Bruin who has informed me that because the situation is getting worse down at the bottom of the trail, we're pulling out."

"But we've got the dinks in a straight up fight. Can't we just keep hitting them?"

"Too hot. We're in danger of being surrounded. The situation is FUBAR."

Eddie nodded his acknowledgment, then heard a familiar voice call out, "Are you a sight for sore eyes!"

Zielinski and Eddie turned to see Tom who, in the standard crouched run of a soldier in a war zone, arrived beside them with boxes of ammunition in each hand. He was grinning from ear to ear, a strange site in the middle of a battle. Tom doled out his ammo. "Get it while it's hot," he said jokingly but stopped his lighthearted banter when he registered the state of Eddie's uniform and his bandaged hand. "How bad is it?" he asked, hoping his friend was not going to lose his hand.

"Bayonet. Should be able to get it patched up. Hurts like hell, though."

"We're heading back down," Zielinski said to Tom.

"Why? It's not just me humping ammo up the hill. We can still fight."

"The fighting is getting bad at base camp," explained the sergeant.

"I've just come from there. Surely, they can hold. Mo's there to make certain they all fight like real men."

Zielinski smiled. "They said on the radio that there was a crazy black soldier with a shotgun running from squad to squad. Guess Mo has just become the all-American hero, whether he likes it or not. He'll probably get the DSC," he added while reloading his M16.

"They'll need to keep the rear open long enough for us to get back there," Eddie said nervously.

"They'll hold," Tom said decisively, but inwardly, he began to panic. His company had never been beaten back. He wasn't used to retreating. Then there was the promise he had made. How could he carry out Skoberne's dying wish if they were moving down the pathway, away from the summit?

"Sergeant, we're Americans. We don't retreat, and I know the lieutenant would want us to keep pushing on. We're so close."

"Thank you for the pep talk, Moretti, but orders are orders. We are to evacuate the mountain trail and head back to the village." Zielinski could tell Tom was agitated and wanted to say more, but the sergeant was not in the mood to indulge an argument. He stared down Tom until his eyes dropped.

"Can you still fire the pig?" Zielinski said, changing the subject and directing his question to Eddie.

"Yeah, I think so, but I won't be able to carry and shoot," Eddie replied as he fitted a new belt of ammunition to the now bloodstained machine gun.

Tom looked around him and saw men beginning to fall back and give each other covering fire. They were so close to the top, it was maddening. And what of the promise he had made? When would he have a chance to honor it? At that moment, in the midst of combat, he vowed to himself that someday, somehow, when the war was over, he would come back and carry out Lieutenant Skoberne's dying request. "What's up there? Why is it so important that they are throwing everything they've got to stop us, and we are willing to spill so much blood to get there?"

"I don't know, son, but we've got to get out of here before the flyboys napalm the top and strafe this area. He checked his watch. We've got four minutes, so let's move before we become a friendly-fire stat," Zielinski said, pointing to the downward trail.

And so they joined the others of the American companies who were slowly but inexorably peeling down the track, pausing to give cover as they retreated. It was a disciplined pullback, but it still felt like a rout to Tom, a humiliating slinking away from a fight. Skoberne and Alabama were dead. Ortiz was seriously wounded, and now Eddie was hurt. And all for what? Why were they leaving when the enemy was right there in front of them?

Eddie set up his M60 by the big boulder where they had taken cover a day ago, although it felt more like a lifetime ago. Despite his bandages, he was able to get his index finger around the trigger mechanism and, supporting himself with his left arm, fired a burst of covering fire to allow others to extricate themselves from the fight. As the machine gun bucked with recoil, it shook his brutalized hand, but he gritted his teeth as he continued to blast away at the oncoming enemy.

Just then, Tom saw the man they needed most moving down the trail. The doctor saw them coming and said almost flippantly, "What's the injury?"

Tom pointed to Eddie. "He got a bayonet in the hand, but he still needs to use the pig."

"Looks like he's doing fine."

"Come on, Doc, you gotta give him something for the pain."

"Look over at the stretcher," Doc said, pointing at an unconscious man being carried by the two stretcher bearers Tom had had a run-in with earlier. "That man was turned sideways when he was hit. The round left him with a compound fracture of his right thigh bone before the bullet embedded itself in his left. He's lost a pint of blood, and his balls were blown off. He was given the last of my morphine. When he wakes up, that nineteen-year-old will be told that thanks to his service in Vietnam, he's been castrated and will never have a family of his own – and as if that's not enough, it's 50-50 that he'll walk without a cane for the rest of his life!" McCarrick barked angrily.

Tom backed down when he saw Doc's raw emotion. "I'm sorry," Tom apologized in the manner of a schoolboy who had disappointed his favorite teacher.

"No, I'm sorry, Moretti. I'm used to one or two injuries per patrol, but here ..." Doc said, pointing up the menacing track. "...here ... I understand what it means when they talk about 'hell on earth'," he added with a sob of emotion. There was nothing more to be said. Tom nodded his understanding and turned back to Eddie and Zielinski.

At that moment, the shriek of jets echoed around the countryside and, moments later, the top of the trail, now in the distance, exploded into a roiling fireball. The depraved orange, black and yellow clouds blossomed and grew as if the mountain had turned into a volcano to disgorge fire and death.

Tom heard a few soldiers cheer, happy to remind Charlie who really had the power. He knew how they felt, but he didn't join in. Just then, he saw two NVA soldiers on fire burst out of the bushes. They raced toward the Americans as if hoping to outrun the flames that had already engulfed them. Eddie took them down with a burst from his machine gun.

"Why did you do that?" screamed Humby.

"What?" Eddie shouted over the noise of battle.

"Why did you put them out of their misery? Should have let them burn; they deserve it," Humby observed and moved on as if what he had said was as normal as ordering his eggs sunny-side up.

Eddie's eyes followed Humby as he jogged down the path, his necklace of ears swinging from one side to another. Tom had rejoined Eddie and Zielinski. They could hear the exchange of fire below them and, while the napalm had bought them some time, they knew they'd come under pressure from that direction again. The army's current strategy seemed to be out of the frying pan and into the fire.

***

Mo had never been a fan of the Vietnamese language and had no interest in learning it. Everything sounded like inane yammering to him and, right now, he blamed the ARVN troops he was with for not knowing English, rather than seeing that it was not unreasonable for the Vietnamese language to be spoken in Vietnam. The men were terrified and useless just when he needed them to fight, although the simple truth was that they were useless most of the time, nothing special about today. This conflict might be the white man's war, but he was damned if he was going to let a bunch of gooks wipe out both black and white Americans. "Get up and fight, dammit!" he yelled at the men. To no avail.

The soldiers hugged the dirt as if they were about to eat it. Mo stuck his head up and looked down the iron sight of his shotgun. An NVA soldier was crouching by a bush only twenty yards away. He had detected Mo's movement out of the corner of his eye, but before he could respond, he took the full blast of a Stevens Model 77E and dropped to the ground. Mo turned back to the cowering ARVN troops. "That's what you've gotta do, okay?" Mo directed, glaring into the eyes of the man nearest him as he dragged him to his feet. They were more liability than asset. If they hadn't learned basic soldiering in whatever training they'd had, he couldn't do much now.

Mo heard rustling in the undergrowth and raised his shotgun. A man came from around a tree trunk, and Mo nearly tore him in half with his point-blank shot. The enemy soldier fell backward, his arms flailing in the air as his rifle clattered to the ground in a rain of blood. Mo turned to the ARVN troops. "Now do you get it?" he asked.

Mo's competence and aggression were starting to rub off. One of the ARVNs got up and brought his M14 to bear. It was an older rifle, but it had proven reliability. The man scanned the lush green vegetation for a sign of anything alien and spied what he thought was an enemy soldier by a tree branch. He started firing off rounds much to Mo's delight. True, the ARVN soldier had managed only to brutally shoot down the branch rather than a non-existent NVA soldier, but it was better than cowering in a ditch. He slapped the ARVN soldier on the back and gave him a thumbs up.

Now the other members of the ARVN squad wanted to get in on the thumb action. They began firing fairly wildly in the general direction of the enemy and then looked expectantly at Mo for affirmation. Mo smiled to himself and gave them a thumbs up to much-excited chatter and cheering.

They continued to blast away, and Mo headed off to try and build a backbone for another squad. It was clear that Charlie considered this a golden opportunity to surround and wipe out a significant number of American and South Vietnamese forces, and it was down to the men in the rearguard to keep the area as safe as possible for the Americans, including his squadmates, coming off the trail.

The momentum was now so fast that the previous mortar attacks from the NVA had ceased; the Americans were moving faster than they could set them up. In one sense it was a relief; in another, it was embarrassing. It felt like they were being chased off the mountain.

***

Tom splashed through the stream, his M16 in one hand and the M60 in the other. Eddie had been struggling to hold onto it. Zielinski scanned the rear for any NVA intent on getting them before they could get off this cursed trail. A burst of gunfire whizzed past Tom's left ear. He hunched down even further.

"Gimme the pig," growled Eddie, who had taken about three paces on the other side of the stream.

"You sure?" Tom asked, looking at the pain painted across his best friend's face.

"My gun's bigger than you are. Give it to me before you get crushed underneath it," Eddie said, his attempt at a smile turning into a grimace.

Tom handed it over and they padded on down the track, sometimes scrabbling down to relative safety, other times crouching behind cover to fire back at the oncoming hordes of enemy soldiers.

"Grenade!" Zielinski called out as he tossed one toward a bush that was the perfect spot for an enemy soldier to hide in. The grenade detonated with an accompanying scream confirming a kill for the sergeant. They pushed on.

The whine of a round came very close to Tom, who felt it shudder past his left hip. He felt no pain, but then came the sensation that his trousers were wet. He dropped to the ground to check himself.

"I'm hit!" he cried out, more to alert his squadmates than because he felt any fear. Too late for that. Eddie set up his M60 to give covering fire but looked anxiously at Tom whose face was white with worry.

Zielinski slid over to him. "Where are you hit, Moretti?"

Tom pointed to his left hip. "Somewhere there. Doesn't hurt though."

Zielinski turned him over, then threw Tom onto his back and slapped his face. "You fucking idiot!"

"What?" Tom said with wide-eyed horror. How bad was it?

"The gooks shot your canteen. The only thing you're going to die of is dehydration."

Tom could feel himself blushing and looked over at Eddie whose concern had turned into roars of laughter.

"Sorry, sergeant."

"It's okay, understandable given the situation. Now let's keep moving out of this hell hole, shall we?"

"Yes, sir," Tom replied, getting up and moving down the path.

The men were all exhausted but staggered on. They were glad to see that at a particularly narrow part of the trail, a 30 caliber heavy machine gun had been set up on a tripod and was laying down withering fire at the oncoming tide of enemy soldiers. Tom patted the gunner on his back as they passed. "Thank you," was all he could manage but it was heartfelt.

"Keep going! We're about to get out of here ourselves. You have to be one of the last to come down."

Tom nodded.

"What was up there anyway? What was so goddamned important?" the machine gunner asked.

Zielinski was signaling, urging them forward. "I have no idea," Tom replied, still helping Eddie with the M60 as they all continued on. The machine gunner had said out loud what Tom – and everyone else - had been thinking for two days. How many men had been killed or maimed and for what?

Another half hour of ducking and diving, scrabbling and firing got them back under the jungle canopy and onto less steep slopes. But now the sound of gunfire was intensifying. The NVA attempt to outflank the American/ARVN forces was being held in check but continued to rage. The beast of war was still searching for prey.

As the three of them arrived at the base camp, they caught sight of Captain de Bruin on the radio. Hueys coming in to pick up the men were targeting hundreds of NVA soldiers streaming down the trail above them. Several of the choppers had broken off from their mission to evacuate and were engaging targets of opportunity. For the aircrews, it was like shooting fish in a barrel, but de Bruin was trying to get the helicopters to break off. They needed extraction now, and he wasn't sure how long the LZ down by the village would remain viable. He saw Zielinski and knew this was a man he could use. "Sergeant, bring your men and come over here," he called out.

Tom, Eddie and Zielinski made their way over to him. The captain saw the bloody bandages around Eddie's hand. "Soldier, keep heading on to the LZ. Let's get you some help." De Bruin could see that Eddie was about to protest. He had no intention of running away from what was left of his squad. "Son, that's an order," de Bruin said, staring hard at Eddie.

Eddie nodded and looked at Tom and Zielinski. He was about to say something when Zielinski got there first. "Powell, we know. Now get going." Eddie had no option but to turn and make his way down to the waiting choppers. This would be his last day of combat. He was lucky; the bayonet had missed all the tendons in his hand and the bones, too. The wound would take six weeks to heal to an acceptable level, and by then his tour was up. Except for a scar, he would make a full recovery.

"You two," de Bruin continued, "head over to the southeast flank about 300 yards from here. You'll find Jones there doing a fine job of scaring the ARVN boys into some semblance of competence. I'm sure he could do with a hand, but we should be falling back by squad toward the

LZ." The captain's words were drowned out by the screech of incoming jets, and a series of gigantic explosions rocked the men as shock waves, despite being dissipated by distance and vegetation, rippled through them. "Give 'em hell, boys," de Bruin added looking up at the jungle canopy obscuring the fighters from view.

Tom and Zielinski headed off to make their way through the dense foliage. Deep throated explosions boomed overhead signaling the continued annihilation of the NVA forces on the trail. There had been a drop off in the number of contacts coming from that direction, so the enemy was either biding its time or retreating towards cover to escape the air attacks.

There might be air attacks overhead, but there was still plenty of danger on the ground. The two men moved cautiously through the undergrowth, every sense on high alert. Tom moved aside a giant leaf and came across a crouching Vietnamese soldier. The man turned toward them, a look of utter terror on his face as he grasped his rifle. Tom was ready and he was quicker but paused when he realized that the man in front of him was wearing a uniform different from that of the NVA. It looked American, and he was carrying an M14, not an AK47. He was ARVN. Tom lowered his rifle, breathing a sigh of relief that he hadn't just shot an ally and faced a court-martial.

"Good call," Zielinski said, coming up behind Tom.

The moment was shattered by a burst of gunfire not far ahead. The two men strained to see what was going on. Tom moved toward the sound, carefully parted some bushes and was stunned to see Mo lecturing two ARVN soldiers on enfilading fire. The men clearly didn't understand a word he was saying, but through hand gestures and mimicry, they seemed to be getting a vague idea. The three of them aimed their weapons and proceeded to lay down a fierce volley of fire. While Tom couldn't see the outcome, Mo shouted congratulations to one of the men and gave him thumbs up. The ARVN soldier copied this and beamed with pride.

"Worried about your job, sergeant?" Tom said, chuckling.

"That's one of the strangest damned things I've ever seen in an A-O," Zielinski said admiringly. "Private Jones," Zielinski barked as he stepped into the clearing.

Mo looked stunned and surprised when he saw his sergeant coming toward him. The look slowly changed to one of sheepishness mixed with dread. He had no idea what was coming next.

"Yes, sir," Mo gulped.

"Good work, Jones. We are under orders to move to the LZ – now! Can you get your men to fall back safely and not turn this into a rout?"

"I have no idea, sir, and they aren't my men."

"Looks like they are now. Moretti and I will cover you; you get your men behind us," Zielinski ordered.

Mo managed to round up the ARVN squad and organized them to cover Tom and Zielinski's retreat. They moved as a tag team down past the base of the mound which had been the original Viet Cong bunker complex, on past the hinterland between the jungle and the village, and finally into the village itself.

The paddy fields had been transformed into what looked and sounded like a hornet's nest; choppers filled the air with their turbine whines and blasts of downforce. In the distance, trucks were starting to pull out with ARVN forces and their heavy equipment. Body bags were stacked just above the waterline, while the wounded waited their turn to board a Huey. The whole area was alive with the noise and bustle of men with too much to do in too short a time.

Tom looked at the broken and bloodied men and the line of body bags. He knew what he saw was far from the full story; they would have been putting bodies in helicopters from the start of the operation. So many young men in their prime had walked into that jungle and come out spent, damaged and destroyed just a few days later. The cost in terms of money, strategy and lives had been huge. His promise to Skoberne was another casualty of the retreat, and while in the greater scheme of things it amounted to nothing much, to Tom it was a symbol of their overall failure on that mountain path.

Tom turned to Zielinski, saying, "I can't believe we've been through all that, and I haven't got a scratch on me. I've seen so many good men killed or injured, why didn't anything happen to me? Why did I get off the hook so easily?"

"You sure about that?" Zielinski asked.

"What do you mean?"

"Are you sure you've come out of all this undamaged?"

Tom boarded a chopper and flew out of the LZ. Zielinski was right; he was always right.

***

"What became of Mo and your sergeant?" Emily asked.

"Mo became a Black Panther for a while, but that turned into social work, and eventually he got elected to the City Council of Detroit."

"Good for him," Emily said, nodding her approval. She liked the idea of turning sentiments into action.

"As for Staff Sergeant Zielinski, he served for one more tour, but by then things were winding down; he left the army in '75 and went back to Pittsburgh. But, about a year later, in the summer of '76, he was killed when a drunk driver lost control of his car and hit him on the sidewalk."

"That's awful! After everything he went through and survived, he gets killed by a drunk."

"That's life, I guess. Shit happens."

Dusk was coming. The last of the sun's orange fire was just dipping behind the mountains on the horizon, and Tom was standing where he'd last been at the highest point on the track all those years ago.

"How much farther to the summit?" Emily asked.

"Not far, maybe a quarter of a mile. The terrain feels more brutal, but the company is considerably better."

Emily smiled. Things felt more companionable now; they were easier with each other. At the start, she couldn't understand why her grandfather was doing all this, but over the last few days, he had put her through an emotional wringer. Now she got it. She looked at her grandfather and realized that he had been caught between the past and the present. He was physically here with her while he walked with ghosts. This trip allowed him to grieve in a way that hadn't been possible when he was last here, and not when he got home again, when it was important to put Vietnam behind him. The man in front of her was coming to terms with decades' old heartache. Denial, anger, bargaining and depression had all reared their heads over the course of this journey. Would he ever get to acceptance? The answer must lie at the summit. This would be his chance to lay his ghosts to rest, the ones she had never met and her grandmother's, too.

They trudged on, determined to make it to the top before dark. Whatever happened, it would be another night under canvas, but that wasn't a bad thing. The air was fresher here and the stars were coming out as if to greet them. Emily had wanted to test herself, to see what she was made of. She had been in a bar fight, visited an isolated village, tramped through jungle, 'survived' a landmine - she giggled at this - and nearly died on the cliff. But she had also helped to save Ho and had been made a member of his family. Family – her wonderful family and her remarkable grandfather – she was seeing him now with fresh eyes.

And then, they arrived at the top. The sun had gone down, and the night that was always there, just under the cover of day, enveloped them. They used their flashlights to make camp and ate an evening meal in silence. They crawled into their tent and fell asleep within minutes.

***

Emily awoke as dawn was breaking. With no jungle canopy, the light was bright in its early appearance. She felt as if a long arm had reached out and dragged her to this much-anticipated mountain top so that when she got up and opened the tent flap, she expected to see … what? There could never have been a temple or a wise old shaman sitting on a cloud; there were no features to speak of, but the view … she gasped as she looked out over a lush jungle that stretched to the next mountain. The rising sun cast it in majestic purple robes as it reached toward the cloudless sky. "Oh," she exclaimed, completely overwhelmed by the unexpected splendor.

Her grandfather was sitting on the ground a little distance away. He had his back to her, intent on what he was doing. She felt as if this was something she should not disturb, so she crept quietly around him until she saw a small pile of earth beside a hole he had dug. There, in the bottom of it, lay an old lighter, the one that had set off the metal detector in the airport. His head was bowed, and it was clear that he was treating the object with great respect, as if it was a treasure. He was saying something she could not make out when he stopped suddenly, and his shoulders began to shake with sobs.

Emily didn't fully understand what was happening, but she was moved to tears at the sight of her grandfather's anguish and rushed over to embrace him. He hadn't heard her coming but grabbed her and hung on as deep sobs racked his body. They gripped each other as the sobs continued in waves until he reached the bottom of his grief.

Finally, when he was able to speak, Tom croaked, "I'm just a weak old man, sitting on top of a dumb-ass hill because fifty years ago some stupid military types thought it would be a good idea to send a bunch of kids up here to see what was going on. So many decent men died trying to get here, including one who had such confidence we would make it, he asked me to bury his lighter at the top. That promise and his lighter have been a millstone of guilt around my neck ever since. I didn't realize how much it sat heavy on my soul until now. I am sorry I dragged you into this, but I am not sorry you are with me today. We've made this journey all the way together, and I think we understand each other all the better for it."

Emily wiped her eyes and hugged her grandfather again. Then she looked around the summit. "So what was it all about? What's here?"

"It's just a plateau with two trails leading off, but it must have had some kind of strategic importance to the NVA. It probably linked up to the Ho Chi Minh Trail or something. The fact that they were here is what made it important to us, but today, right now, it's just dirt and sky," Tom said, running his fingers through the soil as if to emphasize his point. "Now," he said, looking at the lighter, "now I can finally lay all of that to rest." He paused before continuing. "That's fine for me, but what I need to know is can you forgive me?"

"I didn't want to come with you. I think you knew that. And I didn't like what I heard about your time here - I still don't, but I understand it now, and I am so sorry for the young man who was forced to do things he would never have done in the life he was meant to have. You did what you had to do. If there is any shame, any redemption, then you have made your amends. Long forgives you and his mother forgives you. There is nothing for me to forgive."

Tom looked down at his hands and his grime covered wedding ring. For the first time since Elaine's diagnosis, he knew he would survive. Life's pain and loss would always be there, but if you let them in, they became part of your story.

Now tell me that you are at peace with your past," Emily said and indicating the lighter, "and that you forgive yourself."

Tom nodded. "It's over."

Just then, the first shards of sunlight broke free from the horizon and glinted off the lighter. It shone brightly as if acknowledging the fulfillment of a promise. There was nothing but silence and light as they looked out over the stunning view. It was a beautiful day.

The History

This Vietnam novel is not the true story of any one man, but most of the wartime incidents come from the experiences of those who were there (including the incident when 'Zielinski' puts his hand in the fire). So, while Tom is not any one person, he is, in a sense, every man who fought in the jungles of Vietnam.

The historical events portrayed are a matter of record brought to life by a number of interviews with veterans of the war. Journals, letters and personal accounts have also played a part in my research. Now the race is on to capture the memories of these veterans before they are lost in the mists of time.

What many great war stories (books or films) have in common is that they are set at the time of the conflict. When speaking to the Vietnam vets, now in their seventies, I realized that there was a story to be told about the aftermath, about the fallout of that war on the lives of the men who returned (as well as on the lives of the Vietnamese people, which deserves a book of its own). While concessions to fiction have been made, they have been done in an attempt to make the events and the characters feel immediate and authentic.

Echoes is my attempt to examine ways in which the war shaped some of the troops who came home. The young soldiers of Vietnam had their youths squandered by successive US governments which determined that America should continue to fight a war it should never have fought and, ultimately, could not win. The impact of that policy persisted long after the war ended.

Echoes is my tribute to the those who fought and those who fell. To the extent that I have fallen short, I apologize.

Printed in Great Britain
by Amazon